VAMPIRE MOON

MOON

/ / / /

J.R. RAIN

THE VAMPIRE FOR HIRE SERIES

Published by
Crop Circle Books
212 Third Crater, Moon

Printed in the United States of America.

ISBN-13: 978-1544895970
ISBN-10: 1544895976

Dedication

To Susanna, the bravest girl I know.

Acknowledgments

To Sandy Johnston (again!) and Eve Paludan for helping me look a little smarter than I really am, and to Elaine Babich, always my first reader.

"The devil's in the moon for mischief."
—*Lord Byron*

"We have become one with the Moon and the Sun."
—*Diary of the Undead*

Chapter One

I was alone in my hotel room.

The thick curtains were tightly drawn, and I was watching Judge Judy publicly humiliate this loser slumlord when my cell phone vibrated. I absently rooted through a small mound of Kleenex's on the nightstand until I found my cell. I glanced at the faceplate: unknown number. I briefly debated ignoring the call. After all, Judge Judy nearly had this jerk in tears—and I just love it when she reduces jerks to tears—but I figured this might be a job, and I needed the work. After all, this hotel room didn't pay for itself.

I muted Judge Judy's magnificent rant and flipped open the cell. "Moon Agency."

"Is this the Moon Agency?" asked a male voice.

"Would be a hell of a coincidence otherwise."

There was a long pause. On the other end of the

line, I could hear the caller breathing deeply, probably through his open mouth. His voice had sounded nasally. If I had to guess, I would guess he had been crying.

"Are you, you know, a detective or something?"

"Or something," I said. "How can I help you?"

He paused again. I sensed I was about to lose him, and I knew why. He had been expecting a man. Sadly, I was used to this sort of bias in this business. In reality, most women make better detectives. I waited.

"You any good?"

"Good enough to know you have been crying," I said. I looked at the balled up tissues next to my night stand. "And if I had to guess, I would say there's about a half dozen used Keenixes next to you."

I heard a sound on his end. It was sort of a snort. "You're good."

"It's why I get paid the big bucks. I have a list of references, if you want them."

"Maybe," he said. More wet breathing. I heard a rustling sound, wiping his nose, no doubt. "Look, I just need help. I don't know who else to turn to."

"What kind of help?"

"Better if we don't talk about it over the phone."

"Are you in Orange County?" I asked.

"Yes, Irvine."

"I'll meet you in an hour at The Block in Orange. The world's third largest Starbucks is there."

"No shit?"

"Actually, I was using hyperbole. But it's pretty damn big."

He made another snorting sound over the phone and I could almost hear him grin. "Okay," he said, "I'll meet you at what may or may not be the world's third largest Starbucks."

Whoever he was, I liked him already. I told him to look for the dark-haired girl in the wide-brimmed sunhat.

"Sunhat?"

"I like to look fashionable. My goal is to block out the sun for anyone standing within three feet of me."

He laughed. I noticed his was a hollow laugh. Empty. There was a great sadness in him. And it had to do with someone he had lost. My sixth sense was getting stronger, true, but it didn't take a psychic to figure this one out.

"Well, we all need goals," he said. "I'll look for the dark-haired girl in the wide-brimmed sunhat causing her own solar eclipse."

This time I grinned. "Well, moons and eclipses do go hand-in-hand."

He gave me his name, which was Stuart, and I verified his cell number should he fail to find the world's third largest Starbucks and the giant sunhat shading half of Orange County.

Yes, more hyperbole.

We agreed on a time and hung up. I unmuted the TV just as Judge Judy finished publicly

3

dismembering the slum lord. The verdict: he owed his ex-tenant her full deposit.

Yea, for the little people!

I didn't want to get out of bed. In fact, I didn't want to move. The afternoon wasn't optimum time for me. By all rights I should have been sound asleep at this hour, but I had long ago gotten used to getting up at this hour and picking the kids up at school.

Except now I had been banned from picking the kids up at school.

The ban went into place two weeks ago. The monster in me was probably grateful to finally get to sleep in until sunset. But the mommy in me was heartbroken.

And the mommy in me won out in the end.

Prior to a few weeks ago, I used to have to set an alarm clock to wake up on time. An alarm clock turned to its loudest setting and placed as near to my ear as possible.

Now I woke up on my own, at 3:00 p.m., every day. Like clock work.

Up at 3:00 p.m. with no where to go.

And that's usually when I started crying. Not a great way to start your day—or night, in my case.

I wallowed in some more self-pity before finally forcing myself out of bed and into the bathroom. Once there, I proceeded to apply copious amounts of the strongest sunscreen on the market to my face and hands.

Once done, I grabbed my purse, keys and sunhat

and headed for the door. And while I waited for the elevator, I wondered what my kids were up to. I checked the time on my cell phone. They would be home by now with Danny's mom, who watched them every day. No doubt they were doing homework, or fighting over the TV, or fighting over the video games. Or just fighting. I sighed heavily. I even missed their fights.

I would call them tonight, as I did every night at 7 p.m., which was my nightly phone privilege with them. I would tell them I loved them and missed them. They would tell me the same thing. They would tell me about their day, and I would ask what they did during school, and about the time Anthony would launch into another long-winded tale, Danny, my ex-husband listening on the other end of the line, would jump in and tell me my ten minutes were up and to tell the kids to say goodbye. Once we said goodbye, Danny would abruptly hang the phone up for them.

Click.

And I wouldn't hear from them for another 23 hours and 50 minutes. I used to have twenty minutes with them, and then fifteen. And now ten.

I was going to need more Kleenexes.

Chapter Two

I was waiting for Stuart under a wide green awning, sitting as deep in the shade as possible, as the sun was mercifully beginning to set behind the shining dome of the nearby cineplex.

The Block in Orange is a hip and happening outdoor mall that seemed to appeal mostly to groups of fifteen-year-old girls who spent most of their time doubled over with laughter. Looking at the girls, I was reminded of my daughter. These days, she didn't spend much time doubled over in laughter. These days, she seemed to be sinking deeper into a depression.

Nine years old is too young for a depression.

Suddenly depressed myself, I spotted a man coming around a corner, moving determinedly. He scanned the busy Starbucks crowd, spotted me, and then moved my way. Speaking of shiny domes, the man was completely bald and apparently proud of it. As he got closer, I noted his slacks and tee shirt were badly wrinkled. A thin film of sweat glistened off his head. He wore a cell phone clipped at his hip that looked like it was from the late nineties.

"Samantha Moon?" he asked.

"What an amazing guess," I said.

He looked at my hat.

He said, "Not as amazing as you might think. It's hard to miss that thing."

I usually avoid shaking hands. People tend to recoil when they touch my cold flesh. But Stuart held out his and I reluctantly shook it. Although he flinched slightly, he didn't make an issue out of it, which I was grateful for. As we shook, I also got a strong psychic hit from him. Something bad had happened to him. No. Something bad had happened to someone close to him. And recently. I looked at his other hand. He was wearing a wedding band.

Something bad has happened to his wife.

"Would you like a coffee?" I asked. "Since we're at the third largest Starbucks in the world."

He looked around us. His bald head shimmered in the sun.

"You weren't kidding. A place this big, you'd think the coffee was damned good."

"Not just good," I corrected. "This is Starbucks. Their coffee is magical."

"It sure as hell can make five bucks disappear. Seven bucks if you get all that foo-foo crap."

"Foo-foo crap?"

"You know, whipped cream and syrup and

something called java chips."

"Oh, the yummy foo-foo crap."

He grinned and sat opposite me. He was a small man and slender. His bald head was oddly appealing to me. It was perfectly proportioned. No deep ridges or odd grooves. The skin was lightly tan and even. I thought I might just be looking at the world's most perfect bald head. I wanted to touch it. Bad.

He pointed to my hat.

"So do you always wear such a big hat?" he asked.

I generally deflect personal questions, especially any questions that relate to my...condition.

I said, "It helps with my phone reception."

He looked at me blankly for a second or two, then broke into a smile. "Ah, it looks like a satellite dish, I get it. Funny."

I asked if he wanted some magical coffee and he declined, claiming it was too late in the day to drink coffee. I used that as my excuse, too, although it was only a half-truth. Six years ago, it would have been too late in the day for coffee, but now coffee only made me sick.

"So tell me about your wife," I said. "It's why you're here, isn't it?"

He sat back and crossed his arms over his chest. His eyes narrowed. His pupils shrank.

"Yes, but how did you know about my wife?" he asked.

"Women's intuition."

He studied me some more, then finally shrugged. He sat forward again and rested his small hands loosely on the table in front of him.

"My wife was killed about a month ago."

"I'm sorry to hear that."

"So am I," he said.

He told me about it. She had died in a local plane crash. She, and nine others. The plane had flown into the side of the San Bernardino Mountains not too far from here. No survivors. I recalled reading about it on the internet, but the story had not been followed up on in the news, and I had no idea why the plane crashed or where the investigators were in their investigation. It had been a big story that turned quickly into a non-story. I smelled a cover-up.

I don't think I had ever known anyone who had lost someone in a plane crash. I recalled Stuart's words from a few minutes earlier: *She was killed.* Not: *She was in an accident.*

"I'm sorry," I said again when he was finished.

He nodded. Talking about his wife dying in a plane crash had sombered him. Had I known him a little better, I would have reached out and took his hand. As it was, all I could offer were some sympathetic noises and the occasional sorry. Both seemed inadequate.

We were silent for a few more seconds and when the time seemed appropriate, I said, "You don't think the crash was an accident."

"No."

"You think someone killed her."

"I *know* someone killed her. She was murdered. And so was everyone else on board."

***

An elderly couple sat next to us with their books of crossword and sudoku puzzles. Both sipped quietly from tall cups of coffee. In Starbucks speak, tall cups were, of course, small cups.

I studied Stuart. I wasn't sure what to think about him. My sixth sense didn't know what to make of him either. He seemed sane enough, although terribly grief-stricken. The grief-stricken part was what worried me. Grief-stricken always trumped sane.

With the elderly couple nearby, Stuart and I automatically lowered our voices and moved a little closer.

I asked, "Why do you think she was murdered?"

"She had received multiple death threats prior to the plane crash, she and everyone else on board."

Okay, sanity was gaining. But I had questions. Serious questions.

"Why would someone threaten your wife's life, and the others on board?"

"They were going to testify in court. She, and five or six other witnesses."

Stuart unconsciously reached for something that wasn't there. As it was, his fingers closed on empty air. I suspected I knew what they were reaching for:

something alcoholic and strong. Unfortunately, we were at a Starbucks, and as far as I knew, they didn't serve any whiskeyaccinos. At least not yet.

"At the time of the crash, she was with the other witnesses?"

"Yes," he said. "They were being flown to a safe house at the Marine base in Camp Pendleton. At the time, of course, I hadn't known where the government was flying her to. I do now."

"Who was she going to testify against?"

Stuart looked at me hesitantly. I sensed I knew the source of his hesitancy. He was about to involve me in something extremely dangerous. He wasn't sure if he should. Here I was, a cute gal wearing an urban sombrero, and no doubt he didn't want to put me in harm's way.

"You can tell me," I said. "I'm a helluva secret keeper."

He shook his head.

"Maybe I should just let this go," he said.

"Maybe," I said. "But I'm a big girl."

"These people are extremely dangerous and, as you can see, can strike anywhere."

"You caught the 'big girl' part, right?"

"It's going to take more than being a big girl, Samantha. It's going to take an army, I'm afraid."

"Call me Sam. And there's very little that I fear."

He squinted, studying me, and as he did so his perfect bald head caught some of the setting sun. There's beauty everywhere, I thought, even in baldness.

"You're really not afraid, are you?" he asked.

"Nope."

"You should be."

"I'm afraid of a lot of things, but men with big guns aren't one of them. My kids' math homework, well, that's another story."

He grinned.

"Fine," he said. "But don't say I didn't warn you."

"Duly noted."

He looked at me some more. He didn't know what to do with his empty hand. It opened and closed randomly. No doubt he was used to holding his wife's hand. Now, I suspected, her hand had been replaced by a crystal tumbler of the hard stuff.

"She was going to testify against Jerry Blum."

I nodded. I knew the name, especially since I had once been a federal agent. Jerry Blum had single-handedly built an enormous criminal empire that stretched down into Mexico and as far up as Canada, which was no surprise since he was, of all things, Canadian. These days he worked hard to bring drugs to the streets and schools of Orange County. Six years ago, he had dabbled in home loan scams, which had been my specialty. He had an uncanny knack of distancing himself from anything illegal, and an even more uncanny knack to avoid prosecution, which is why my department never caught him.

Last I heard, he had been standing trial for a

bizarre crime outside a nightclub in Seal Beach, California, where Jerry Blum had uncharacteristically lost his cool and popped someone with a handgun. Yes, witnesses were everywhere.

I asked Stuart about this, and he confirmed that his wife had indeed been one of the witnesses. She had seen the whole thing, along with five others. She had agreed to testify to what she saw, thus putting her life in mortal danger.

I tapped my longish fingernail on the green plastic table. My fingernails tended to come to a point these days, but most people seemed not to notice, and if they did, they didn't say anything about it. Maybe they were scared of the weird woman with pointed fingernails.

I said, "Why do you think Jerry Blum was involved in your wife's plane crash?"

"Because as of today he is a free man. No witnesses, and thus no case. It's been ruled self-defense."

"But we're talking about a *plane crash*, and if the plane was headed to a military base, then we're probably talking about a military aircraft."

"I know I sound crazy, but look at the facts. Jerry Blum has a history of silencing witnesses. This case was no different. Just a little more extravagant. Witnesses silenced, and Blum's a free man."

I continued tapping. People just didn't take down military aircrafts. Even powerful people. But the circumstantial evidence was compelling.

Whoops! I was tapping too hard. Digging a hole in the plastic. Whoops. A vampiric woodpecker.

I asked, "So what have federal investigators determined to be the cause of the crash?"

"No clue," said Stuart. "The investigation is still ongoing. Every agency on earth is involved in it. I've been personally interviewed by the FBI, military investigators and the FAA."

"Why you?"

"No clue," he said again. "But I think it's because they suspect foul play."

I nodded but didn't tap.

Stuart added, "But he killed her, Sam. I know it, and I want you to help me prove it. So what do you say?"

I thought about it. Going after a crime lord was a big deal. I would have to be careful. I didn't want to jeopardize my family or Stuart. Myself I wasn't too worried about.

I nodded and he smiled, relieved. We discussed my retainer fee. We discussed, in fact, a rather sizable retainer fee, since this was going to take a lot of time and energy. He agreed to my price without blinking and I gave him my PayPal address, where he would deposit my money. I told him I would begin once the funds had been confirmed. He understood.

We shook hands again and, once again, he barely flinched at my icy grip. And as he walked away, with the setting sun gleaming off his shining dome, all I wanted to do was run my fingers over his perfect bald head.

I needed to get a life.

Chapter Three

A half hour later, I was sitting in a McDonald's parking lot and waiting for 7:00 p.m. to roll around.

I had already concluded that traffic was too heavy for me to get back to my hotel in time to call my kids, and so I decided to wait it out here, just off the freeway, with a view of the golden arches and the smell of French fries heavy in the air.

My stomach growled. I think my stomach had short-term memory loss. French fries were no longer on the menu.

The sun was about to set. For me, that's a good thing. The western sky was ablaze in fiery oranges and reds and yellows, a beautiful reminder of the sheer amount of smog in southern California.

I checked the clock on the dash: 6:55.

My husband Danny made the rules. We had no official agreement regarding who could see the kids when. It was an arrangement he set up outside of the courts, because in this case he was judge, jury and executioner. A month or so ago he threatened to expose me for who I am, claiming he had evidence, and that if I fought him I would never see the kids again. Danny was proving to be far more ruthless than I ever imagined. Gone was the gentle husband I had known, replaced by something close to a monster of his own.

Not the undead kind. Just the uncaring kind.

For now, as hard as it was not seeing my kids, I played by his rules, biding my time.

I drummed my fingers on the steering wheel. A small wind made its way through my open window, now bringing with it the scent of cooking beef. Maybe some McNuggets, too. I sniffed again. And fries, always the fries.

I looked at my watch. Three minutes to go. If I called early, Danny wouldn't answer. If I called late, then tough shit, 7:10 was my cut-off no matter what time I called. And if I called past 7:10, he wouldn't pick up. Again, shit out of luck. The calling too late thing had only happened once, when I was in a client meeting. I vowed it wouldn't happen again, clients be damned.

Two minutes to go. I treasured every second I had with my kids, and I hated Danny for doing this to me. How could he turn on me like this?

Easy, I thought. *He's afraid of you. And when people are afraid they do evil, hurtful things.*

One minute. I rolled up my window. I wanted to be able to hear my kids. I didn't want some damn

Harley coming by and drowning out little Anthony's comically high-pitched voice, or Tammy's too-serious recounting of that day's school lessons.

Thirty seconds. I had my finger over the cell phone's send button, Danny's home number—my *old* home number—already selected from my contact list and ready to go.

Ten seconds. Outside, somewhere beyond the nearby freeway's arching overpass, the sun was beginning to set and I was beginning to feel good. Damn good. In fact, within minutes I was about to feel stronger than I had any right to feel.

And I was about to talk to my kids, too. A smile that I hadn't felt all day touched my lips.

At 7:00 p.m. on the nose, I pushed the *send* button. The phone rang once and Danny picked up immediately.

"The kids aren't here," he said immediately in his customary monotone.

"But—"

"They're with Nancy getting some ice cream."

Nancy was, of course, the home-wrecker. His secretary fling that had become more than a fling. The name of that witch alone nearly sent me into a psychotic rage.

"They're with *her*?"

"Yes. They like her. We all do."

"When will they be back?"

"I don't know, and that's none of your concern."

"So when can I call back?"

"You can call back tomorrow at seven."

"That's bullshit, Danny. This was my time with—"

"Tomorrow," he said, and hung up.

Chapter Four

An hour later, I was boxing at a little sparring club in downtown Fullerton, a place called Jacky's. Jacky himself trained me, which was a rare honor these days, as the little Irishman was getting on in years. I think he either had a crush on me, or didn't know what the hell to make of me, since I tended to destroy his boxing equipment.

The sun had set an hour ago and I was at maximum strength. I was also still pissed off at Danny, hurt beyond words, and now the old Irishman was feeling the brunt of it.

He was wearing brand-new punch mitts, which were those little protective pads trainers use to cover their hands. I was leveling punch after punch into his mittened hands, sometimes so rapidly that my hands were a blur even to my eyes.

And I wasn't just punching them, I was hitting them hard. Perhaps too hard.

Jacky was a tough guy, even though he was pushing sixty. He was an ex-professional boxer back in Ireland who had suffered his share of broken noses, and no doubt had broken a few noses himself. I had never known him to show pain or any sign of weakness. And so when he began wincing with each punch, I knew it was time to ease up on the poor guy. He was far too tough and stubborn to lower the gloves himself and ask for a break.

I paused in mid-strike and said, "Let's take a break."

To say that Jacky was relieved would have been an understatement.

Still, he shot back. "Is that all you got, wee girl?" he asked loudly, and, I think, for the benefit of anyone watching, since I sometimes attracted a crowd of curious onlookers, and Jacky had a tough-guy image to uphold.

Of course, I never wanted to attract crowds of onlookers, as I generally avoid bringing attention to myself. But since that incident last month with a Marine boxer, an incident in which I put him in a hospital, well, I had become somewhat of a hero in this mostly women's boxing club.

"Well, I could probably go another round or two," I said lightly to Jacky.

"I'll pretend I didn't hear that," he said.

Jacky shook off the protective gloves. His hands were ruddier than his Irish complexion; his fingers were fat and swollen.

"Sorry about that," I said. "I had a bad night."

"I'd hate to get on your bad side."

"Doesn't seem to worry my ex-husband."

"Then I say he's not right in the head. You punch like a hammer." He shook his head in wonder. I often caused this reaction from the old boxer, who hadn't yet figured me out. "Harder than anyone I've ever trained, man or woman."

"Yeah, well, we've all got our talents," I said. "Yours, for example, is having red hair."

"That's not a talent."

"Close enough."

He shook his head and held up his red hands which, if I looked hard enough at them, I could probably see throbbing.

"I need to soak these in ice," he said. "But if I soak these in ice, the women here will think I'm a pussycat."

I leaned over and kissed him on his sweating forehead. The blush that emanated from him was instant, spreading from his balding head, down into his neck.

"But you are a pussycat," I said.

"Well, you're a freak of nature, Sam."

Jacky, of course, didn't realize how freaky I was. In fact, I could count on one hand the number of people who knew how freaky I was.

"You could be a world champion," he said. Now we were making our way over to the big punching bag.

"I'm too old to be a world champion," I said. Jacky was always trying to get me to fight professionally.

He snorted. "You're, what, thirty?"

"Thirty-one, and thank you."

However, Jacky was closer than he thought. I was indeed thirty-seven calendar years old, but I was frozen in a thirty-one year old's body.

The age I was when I was attacked.

Granted, if a girl had to pick an age to be immortalized in, well, thirty-one would probably be near the top of her list.

And what happens ten years from now when you're forty-seven but still look thirty-one? Or when your daughter is thirty-one and you still look thirty-one?

I didn't know, but I would cross that bridge when I got there.

Jacky took up his position behind the punching bag. "So what's eating at you anyway, Sam?"

"Everything," I said. I started punching the bag, moving around it as if it were an actual opponent, using the precise body movements Jacky had taught me. Ducking and weaving. Jabs. Hooks. Hard straight shots. Punches that would have broken jaws and teeth and noses. Jacky bared his teeth and absorbed the punches on the other side of the bag like the champion he was, or used to be. I took a small breather. So did Jacky. Sweat poured from my brow.

"Let me guess," said Jacky, gasping slightly, and looking as if he had taken actual physical shots to his own body. "Is it that no-good ex-husband of yours?"

"Good guess."

"Does he realize you could kick his arse from here to Dublin?"

"He realizes that," I said. "And why Dublin?"

"National pride," he said. "So why don't you go kick his fucking arse?"

"Because kicking ass isn't always the answer, Jacky."

"Works for me," he said.

"We'll call that *Plan B*."

"Would be my *Plan A*. A good arse-kicking always clears the air."

I laughed. "I'll keep it in mind."

"Break's over. Hands up."

He leaned back into the bag and I unleashed another furious onslaught. Pretending the bag was my ex-husband was doing wonders for me.

"You're sweating like a pig, Sam," screamed Jacky. "I like that!"

"You like pig sweat?"

He just shook his head and screamed at me to keep my fists up. I grinned and unleashed a flurry of punches that rocked the bag and nearly sent little Jacky flying, and attracted a small group of women who gathered nearby to watch the freak.

And as I punched and sweated and kept my fists up, I knew that fighting Danny wasn't the answer. Luckily, there were other ways to fight back.

Chapter Five

After a long shower and a few phone calls to some friends working in the federal government, I was at El Torito Bar and Grill in Brea—just a hop, skip and a jump from my hotel.

I was wearing jeans and a turtle neck sweater. Not because it was cold outside, but because I looked so damn cute in turtle neck sweaters. The stiff-looking man sitting across from me seemed to think so, too. Special Agent Greg Lomax, lead investigator with the FBI, was in full flirt mode, and it was all I could do to keep him on track. Maybe I shouldn't have looked so cute, after all.

Damn my cuteness.

El Torito is loud and open. The loudness and openness was actually of benefit for anyone having a private conversation, which was probably why Greg had chosen it.

Personally, I found the noise level here a bit

overwhelming, but then again, I'm also just a sweet and sensitive woman.

It was either that or my supernaturally acute hearing that quite literally picked up every clattering dish, scraping fork, and far ruder sounds best not described. And, of course, picked up the babble of ceaseless conversations. If I wanted to I could generally make out any individual conversation within any room. Handy for a P.I., trust me. Granted, I couldn't hear through walls or anything, but sounds that most people could hear, well, I could just hear that much better.

"Lots of people over at HUD talk very highly of you," he said.

"I gave them the best seven years of my life," I said.

"And then you came down with some sort of, what, rare skin disease or something?"

"Or something," I said.

"Now you work private," he said.

"Yes. A P.I."

"How's that working out?"

"It's good to be my own boss," I said. "Now I give myself weekly pay raises and extra long coffee breaks."

He grinned. "That's cute. Anyway, I was told to tell you what I could. So ask away. If I can't talk about something, or I just don't know the answer, I'll tell you."

We were sitting opposite each other in a far booth in the far corner of the bar. I was sipping some house zinfandel, and he was drinking a Jack and Coke. White wine and water were about the only two liquids I could consume. Well, that and something else.

Just thinking about that something else immediately turned my stomach.

I said, "So do you think the crash was an accident?"

"You get right to the point," he said. "I like that."

"Must be the investigator in me."

He nodded, drank some more Jack and Coke. "No, this wasn't an accident. We know that much."

"How do you know that?"

He smiled. "We just know."

"Okay. So how did the plane crash?"

"All signs point to sabotage."

"Sabotage how?"

He was debating how much to tell me. I could almost see the wheels working behind his flirtatious eyes. No doubt he was computing the amount of information he could still give me and still not give up any real government secrets, and yet leave me satisfied enough to sleep with him tonight. A complex formula for sure.

Men are better at math than they realize.

He said, "Someone planted a small explosive in the rudder gears. The pilot heard the explosion, reported it immediately, and then reported that he had lost all control of the plane. Ten minutes later the plane crashed into the side of the San

Bernardino Mountains."

"And everyone on board was killed?"

"Yes. Instantly."

"Is there any reason to believe that these key witnesses were killed to keep them from testifying?"

"There is every reason to believe that. It's the only motive we have." He drank the rest of his Jack and Coke. "Except there's one problem: our number one suspect was in jail at the time of the crash."

The waiter came by and dropped off another drink for Greg. Perhaps the waiters here at El Torito Bar and Grill were psychic. Greg picked up his drink and sipped it.

"It would take a lot of pull to sabotage a military plane," I said.

"Not as much as you might think," said Greg. "This was a DC-12, and the contract the government has with them stipulates that the makers of the planes get to use their own mechanics."

"So the mechanic was a civilian."

"Yes."

"Have you found the mechanic?"

"Yeah," he said. "Dead in his apartment in L.A."

"How did he die?"

"Gunshot in the mouth."

"Suicide?"

"We're working on it."

I followed up with this some more, but Greg

seemed to have reached the limit of what he was willing to tell me.

Greg motioned to my half-finished drink. "You going to finish that?"

"Probably not."

"You want to head over to my place and, you know, talk some more about what it's like giving yourself raises?"

I said, "When you say 'talk' don't you really mean boff my brains out?"

He grinned and reddened. I reached over and patted his superheated face.

"You'll just have to give yourself a raise tonight," I said, and left him my card. "Call me if you hear anything new."

"But I live right around the cor—"

"Sorry," I said. "But your calculations were off."

I smiled sweetly and left.

Chapter Six

We were at the beach, sitting on the wooden deck of a lifeguard tower. The sign on the lifeguard tower said no sitting on the wooden deck.

"We're breaking the law," I said.

Kingsley Fulcrum turned his massive head toward the sign above us. As he did so, some of the moonlight caught his cheek bones and strong nose and got lost somewhere in the shaggy curls that hung on his beefy shoulders.

"We are risking much to be here," he said. "If we get caught, our super secret identities may be discovered."

I said, "Especially if I show up invisible in the mug shot."

Kingsley shook his head.

"You vampires are weird," he said.

"This coming from a guy who howls at every

full moon."

He chuckled lightly as a small, cold wind scurried over my bare feet. Before us, the dark ocean stretched black and eternal. Small, frothing whitecaps slapped the shore. In the far distance, twinkling on the curve of the horizon, were the many lights of Catalina Island. Between us and Catalina were the much brighter lights of a dozen or so oil rigs. The beach itself was mostly quiet, although two or three couples were currently smooching on blankets here and there. They probably thought they were mostly hidden under the cover of darkness. They probably hadn't accounted for a vampire with built-in night vision watching them. A gyrating couple, about two hundred feet away up the beach, might have been doing the nasty.

Kingsley turned to me. I always liked the way the bridge of his nose angled straight up to his forehead. Very Roman. And very hot.

He said, "You became a private investigator after you were changed?"

"Yes."

"So that means you took your P.I. photo when you were a vampire."

"Yes."

"So how did you manage that?"

"I wore a lot of make up that day," I said smugly, proud of myself. I had wondered what to do about the photo, too.

"So the make up showed up, even though you

didn't?"

"Yes, exactly. I even made sure I blinked when the picture was taken."

"Just in case your eye sockets came up empty."

"Exactly."

"You could have worn colored contacts," said Kingsley.

"But then the whites of my eyes would have come up empty," I said.

He nodded. "So you sacrificed your vanity."

"I might look like a major dork in the picture, but at least I look human. Granted, if you look close enough, there is a blank spot somewhere near my throat, where I had missed a patch of skin, but not too many people are looking at my throat."

"No," said Kingsley. "They're looking at the dork with her eyes closed."

I punched him in the arm. The force of my blow knocked him sideways.

"Ouch!" He rubbed his arm and grinned at me, and the light from the half moon touched his square teeth. Kingsley was a successful defense attorney in Orange County. A few months ago, he had hired me to investigate a murder attempt on his life. His case had come at a difficult time in my life. Not only had I just caught my husband cheating, the bastard had the gall to kick me out of my own home.

A very difficult time, to say the least. The wounds were still fresh and I was still hurting.

And I would be for a very long time.

Not the greatest time to start a new romance

with a hunky defense attorney with massive shoulders and a tendency to shed.

"There are two people boffing over there," said Kingsley, looking off over his shoulder. "I think one of their names is *Oh, Baby.*"

Kingsley's hearing was better than mine, which was saying something.

I grinned and elbowed him. "Will you quit eavesdropping."

He cocked his head to one side, and said, "I was wrong. His name is *Oh, God.*"

I elbowed him again, and we sat silently some more. Our legs were touching. His thigh was about twice as wide as mine. We were both wearing jeans and sweaters.

I sensed Kingsley's desire to touch me, to reach out and lay his big hand over my knee. I sensed him forcibly controlling himself.

Down boy.

I was still looking out over the black ocean, which, to my eyes, wasn't so black. The air shimmered with light particles which flashed and streaked across the night sky. I often wondered what these streaking lights were. I didn't know for sure, but I had a working hypothesis. I suspected I was seeing the physical manifestation of energy itself. Perhaps I was being given a behind-the-scenes glimpse of the workings of our world.

Then again, I've been wrong before.

Kingsley was still looking at me, still fighting what he most wanted to do. And what he most wanted to do was ravage me right here and now on this lifeguard pier. But the brute held himself in check. Smart man. After all, I gave him no indication that I wanted to be ravaged.

"Not yet, Kingsley," I said calmly, placing my own hand lightly on his knee. "I'm not ready yet."

He nodded his great, shaggy head, but said nothing. I sensed his built-up energy dissipate in an instant. Hell, I could practically see it zigzagging away from his body, caught up by the lunar wind and merging with the silver spirits surfing the California night skies.

He exhaled and sort of deflated. Poor guy. He had gotten himself all worked up. He rested his own hand lightly on mine, and if my own cold flesh bothered him, he didn't show it.

And while we sat there holding hands, with me soaking in the tremendous warmth of his oversized paw, I told him about my latest case.

When I was finished, he said, "Jerry Blum is a dangerous man."

"I'm a dangerous girl."

From far away, emerging from under the distant Huntington Beach Pier, was a lone jogger. Even from here, the jogger appeared to be a very big man. The man was easily a hundred yards away.

Kingsley, who had been looking down at my leg, suddenly cocked his head, listening. He then turned and spotted the jogging man. The man, as far as I could tell, wasn't making a sound.

I was intrigued. "You heard him?"

"Yes and no," said Kingsley, still looking over his shoulder at the approaching man. "But I could hear his dog."

I looked again. Sure enough, running along at the man's feet, about the size of a rat on steroids, was something small and furry. A dog, and it looked miniscule next to the running man. I smiled. For some reason, I found it heartwarming to see such a big man running with such a little doggie.

Kingsley said, "So what, exactly, is your client hiring you to do? Does he want you to take down one of the most dangerous criminals on the West Coast?"

"Taking him down will be extra."

"Taking him down will be dangerous for both you and your family, Sam. Remember, this guy doesn't play nice."

"I won't put my family in harm's way," I said. "And besides, who says I play nice, either? I've been known to bite."

"Very funny. But I don't like this, Sam. This isn't your typical P.I. gig. Hell, the FBI still hasn't figured out a way to nail this guy, and you're just one woman."

"But a helluva woman."

"Sure, but why am I more concerned about your safety than you are?" he asked.

"Because you like me a little," I said, blinking daintily.

"I would like you more if you stayed away from this case."

Something small and furry and fat suddenly appeared in the sand beneath our feet. It was the same little dog, now trailing a leash. It was, in fact, a tea cup Pomeranian, and it was about as cute as cute gets. Maybe even cuter. It wagged its tail a mile a minute and turned in a half dozen small circles, creating a little race track in the sand. It never once took its eyes off Kingsley.

"It likes you," I said.

"Go figure."

Kingsley made a small noise in his throat and the little dog abruptly sat in the sand in front of him, staring, panting, wagging.

And from out of the darkness, sweating through a black tee shirt and rippling with more muscle than two or three men put together—that is, if those men weren't Kingsley—was the same tall man we had seen a few minutes earlier. He approached us with a small limp that didn't seem to bother him.

"Kill, Ginger," said the man easily, grinning. Ginger turned in two more circles and sat before Kingsley again. The man reached down and gently patted its little head. "Good girl." He looked up at us. "Were you two at least a little afraid for your lives?"

"Terrified," said Kingsley.

"I might have wet myself a little," I said.

The man stood straight and I might have seen his six-pack through his wet tee shirt. *Hubba, hubba.*

"She doesn't usually come up to strangers," said

the man. "In fact, I'm fairly certain she's terrified of her own shadow. Of course, it's a pretty fat shadow. Scares me a little, too."

Kingsley slipped off the wooden platform, landing softly in the sand, too softly for a man his size. Ginger didn't move, although her tail might have started wagging at close to the speed of light. The attorney reached down and scratched the little dog between turgid ears. Ginger, if anything, looked like a star-crossed teenager at a rock concert. Or me at a Stones concert.

"Okay, that's a first," said the man, looking genuinely surprised. "Took me three months before I was anywhere near those ears."

Kingsley, still petting the dog, said, "She probably had a bad experience when she was a pup. If I had to guess, I would say she was beaten and abused before she found her new home. Probably by a man about your size, and so she doesn't like men, but she does like you, even though you run too fast for her little legs, and you don't give her near enough treats." Kingsley gave Ginger a final pat and stood. "Like I said, it's just a guess."

"Good guess. And spot on. She had been abused before my girlfriend rescued her. Of course, there was no rescuing the man who abused her. Let's just say when I was done with him, he had a newfound respect for every living creature."

Kingsley and I grinned. I had no doubt that the man in front of us could have inflicted some serious damage on someone.

He went on, "And if I gave Ginger any more treats I would have to roll her on my runs."

I snickered and Kingsley laughed heartily. He reached out a hand. "I know you from somewhere."

"Not the first time I've heard that," said the man as he scooped up the little dog, who promptly disappeared behind a bulging bicep muscle that had my own eyes bulging.

Kingsley's eyes narrowed. His thinking face. "You used to play football for UCLA."

"Is there any other school?"

The attorney snapped his fingers. "You were on your way to the pros until your broke your leg."

"Don't you just hate when that happens?" said the man lightly. "And you are, of course, Kingsley Fulcrum, famed defense attorney and internet sensation."

Kingsley laughed; so did I. Indeed, a few months ago, someone had tried to kill the attorney outside of a local courthouse. It was a bizarre and humorous incident that had been captured on film and seen around the country, if not the world. *Kingsley, the man who couldn't die.* The world watched as his assailant shot him point-blank five times in the head and neck.

The two men chitchatted for a bit, and I realized, upon closer inspection, that both men were exactly the same height. Although the stranger was muscular and powerful-looking, Kingsley had a beefy savagery to him that no man could match. Even ex-football players.

After all the silly football talk, I soon learned that the tall stranger now worked as a private eye. I perked up. Kingsley mentioned I was one, too, and the man nodded and reached into his sweat pants pocket and pulled out a brass card holder. He opened it, gave me one of his cards.

He said, "You ever need any extra help or muscle, call me. I can provide both."

I looked at the card. Jim Knighthorse. I might have heard the name before, perhaps on some local newscast or something. On his card was a picture of him smiling, really cheesin' it up for the camera. I had a very strong sense that Mr. Knighthorse just might have been in love with himself.

"Helluva picture," he said, winking. "If I do say so myself."

I was right.

Chapter Seven

It was far too early in the morning for me, but I didn't care.

The sun was high and hot, and I was sitting in my minivan in the parking lot of my children's elementary school near downtown Fullerton, where I had parked under a pathetic jacaranda tree. The tree was mostly bare but offered some shade.

Beggars can't be choosers.

I was huddled in my front seat, away from any direct sunlight, the shades pulled down on both the driver's side and passenger's side windows. My face was caked with the heaviest sunblock available on the market. Thin leather gloves covered my hands, and I was wearing another cute wide-brimmed sunhat, which sometimes made driving difficult. I had many such hats—all purchased in the last six years, of course—and all a necessity to keep me alive.

And what happens if I'm ever exposed to any direct sunlight?

I didn't know, and I didn't want to find out, either. All I knew was that the sun physically hurts me, even when I'm properly protected. I suspected I would wither and die. Probably painfully, too.

So much for being immortal.

Immortality with conditions.

As I huddled in my seat, I thought about those words again: *wither and die.*

You know, I used to lead a normal life. I grew up here in Orange County, was a cheerleader and softball player, went to college in Fullerton, got a master's degree in criminal science, and then went on to work for the federal government. Lots of dreams and ambitions. One of them was to get married and start a family. I did that, and more.

Life was good. Life was fun. Life was easy.

If someone had told me that one day my daily To-Do List would consist of the words: *1) Buy extra-duty sunblock. 2) Oh, and see if Norco Slaughterhouse will set up a direct billing...* well, I would have told them to go back to their Anne Rice novels.

I sat in my minivan, huddled in my seat, buried under my sunhat and sunblock, wary of any beam of sunlight, and shook my head and I kept shaking my head until I found myself crying softly in my hands. Smearing my sunscreen.

Damn.

I may not have known what lived in me, and I may not have known the dark lineage of my blood, but I knew one thing for fucking sure. No one was going to keep me from seeing my kids. Not Danny. And not the sun.

I opened my van door and got out.

Chapter Eight

I gasped and stumbled.

I reached a gloved hand out and braced myself on the hot fender of my minivan. Heat from the sheet metal immediately permeated the thin glove. Maybe Stephenie Meyer's vampires had it right. Maybe I should move up to Washington State, in the cold and rain, where gray clouds perpetually covered the skies.

Maybe someday. But not now. I had real-life issues to deal with.

I gathered myself together and strode across the quiet parking lot, filled mostly with teachers' and school administrators' cars. I'm sure I must have looked slightly drunk—or perhaps sick—huddled in my clothing, head down, stumbling slightly.

A small wind stirred my thick hair enough to get a few strands stuck in the copious amounts of sunscreen caked on my face. I ignored my hair. I needed to get the hell out of the sun. And fast.

I picked up my pace as another wind brought to me the familiar scents of cafeteria food. Familiar, as in this was exactly what cafeteria food had smelled like back when I was in elementary school.

After crossing the hot parking lot, I stepped up onto a sidewalk and a moment later I was under an eave, gasping.

Sweet, sweet Jesus.

Keeping to the shade and sliding my hand along the stucco wall to keep my balance, I soon found myself in front of the main office door.

Focus, Sam.

I needed to look as calm and normal as possible. School officials didn't take kindly to crazy-looking parents.

My skin felt as if it were on fire. And all I had done was walk across a school parking lot. I wanted to cry.

No crying.

I sucked in some air, held it for a few minutes—yes minutes—and let it out again. My skin felt raw and irritated. I picked hair out of the heavy sunscreen with a shaking hand, adjusted my sunhat, put a smile on my face, and opened the office door.

Just another mom here to see her kids.

***

A few minutes later, I found myself in the principal's office; apparently, I was in trouble.

Principal West was a pleasant-looking man in his mid-fifties. He was sitting behind his desk with his hands folded in front of him. He wore a white long-sleeved dress shirt with Native American-inspired jade cuff links. As far as I knew, he wasn't Native American.

Principal West had always been kind to me. Early on, just after my attack, he had been quick to work with me. I was given special access to the front of the school when picking up my kids. Basically, I got to park where the buses parked—thus avoiding long lines and sitting in the sun longer than I had to. Good man. I appreciated his kindness.

That kindness had, apparently, come to an end.

"I can't let them see you, Samantha, I'm sorry."

"I don't understand."

"I got a call today from Danny. In fact, I got it just about a half hour ago. Your husband—or ex-husband—says that the two of you have an unwritten agreement that you will not be picking the kids up anymore."

"Yes, but—"

"He also says that you have agreed to supervised visits only. Is this true?"

Principal West was a good man, I knew that, and I could see that this was breaking his heart. I nodded and looked away.

He sighed heavily and pushed away from his desk, crossing his legs. "I can't allow you to see them without Danny being present, Samantha. I'm sorry."

"But I'm their mother."

He studied me for a long time before saying, "Danny also said that you are a potential danger to the kids, and that under no circumstances are you to be alone with them."

I was shaking my head. Tears were running down my face. I couldn't speak.

Principal West went on, "You're very ill, Sam. I can see that. Hell, anyone can see that. How and why you pose a threat to your children, I don't know. And what's going on between you and Danny, I don't know that, either. But I would suggest that before you agree to any more such terms, Sam, that you seek legal counsel first. I have never known you to be a threat. Outside of being sick, I have always thought you were a wonderful mother, but it's not for me to say—"

I lost it right there. I burst into tears and cried harder than I had cried in a long, long time. A handful of secretaries, the receptionist and even the school nurse surrounded me. Principal West watched me from behind his desk, and through my tears, I saw his own tears as well.

He wiped his eyes and got up. He put an arm gently around me and told me how sorry he was, and then escorted me out.

Chapter Nine

I hate all men, I wrote.

Even me?

Are you a man, Fang?

Yes, but I'm a helluva man.

Despite myself, I laughed. I was in my hotel room sitting in the cushioned hotel chair. I should have been comfortable, but I wasn't; the chair's wooden arms were bothering me. Come to think of it, the chair wasn't that comfortable, either. Maybe I should complain to hotel management.

Or maybe I should just calm down, I thought. Even better, maybe I should get myself an apartment somewhere and decorate it with my *own* chairs.

It was a thought, but something I would think about later.

How do I know you're a helluva man? I wrote.

I've never seen a picture of you.
   You'll have to take my word for it.
   The word of a man? Never! :)
   Remember: A helluva a man.
   So you say.
   What's got you so upset tonight, Moon Dance?

Fang was my online confidant. I had met him via an online vampire chatroom years ago, back when chatrooms were all the rage. Nowadays, he and I just chatted through AOL, although we kept our old screen names. His was Fang321, and mine was MoonDance. To date, I had yet to tell him anything too personal, although he has probed repeatedly for more information. Admittedly, I have too. We were both deathly curious about each other, but I had my reasons to not reveal my identity, and, according to him, he did, too. Of course, my reason had been obvious: I admitted to him early on that I was a vampire. To his credit, or, more accurately, a ding to his sanity, he had believed me without reservations.

So I told him about my attempt to see my kids, and how Danny was stymieing me at every turn.

You could always kill him, wrote Fang.

Sometimes I don't know when you're joking.

There was a long pause, and then he wrote, *Of course, I was joking.*

Good. You had me worried.

Still, he wrote. *It would solve all your problems.*

And create a ton more, I wrote, and then quickly added: *I'm not a killer.*

Thus wrote the vampire.

I'm a good *vampire.*

There are some who would say that's an oxymoron.

Why can't I be good, too?

Because it's in your nature to kill and drink blood. Ideally, fresh blood from a fresh kill.

I won't kill anything. I would rather shrivel up and die.

But by not drinking fresh blood you are denying yourself the full powers of your being.

How much more powerful do I need to be? I wrote.

You have no idea.

And how do you know so much about vampires, Fang? You've told me long ago that you are human.

A human with a love for all things vampire.

And why do you love vampires so much, Fang?

I have my reasons.

Will you ever tell me what they are?

Someday.

But not on here.

Exactly, he wrote. *Not on here.*

If not on here, then where? I asked.

That's the million dollar question.

I changed subjects. *So what am I supposed to do about Danny?*

Another long pause. I often wondered what Fang did during these long pauses. Was he going to the bathroom? Answering his cell phone? Sitting back and lacing his fingers behind his head as he thought about what he would write next?

Finally, after perhaps five minutes, his words appeared in the IM box: *Danny has all the leverage.*

I thought about that. Indeed, it had been something that occurred to me earlier, but I wanted to see what Fang had up his sleeve.

Keep going, I wrote.

Maybe it's time for you to take back the leverage.

I agree. Any idea how?

Something will come to you. Hey, how psychic are you these days, Moon Dance?

More than I was a few years ago. Why?

Some psychics use automatic writing for answers.

What's automatic writing?

It's when you sit quietly with a piece of paper and a pen and you ask questions. Sometimes answers come through and your pen just...starts writing.

I laughed.

You're kidding.

No, I'm not. It could be a way for you to find answers, Moon Dance.

Answers to what?

Everything.

I thought about that, and a small feeling stirred in my solar plexus.

So how do I do this?

Research it on the internet.

Okay, I will.

Good. And let me know how it goes. 'Night, Moon Dance.

'Night, Fang.

Chapter Ten

I did research it on the internet.

Normally, I would have scoffed at such nonsense (automatic writing? C'mon!), but my very strange existence alone suggested that I should at least consider it.

And I liked the possibilities. Who wouldn't want spiritual answers, especially someone with my condition?

According to a few sites I checked out on the internet, the process of automatic writing seemed fairly simple. Sit quietly at a table with a pen and paper. Center yourself. Clear your mind. Hold the pen lightly over the paper...and see what comes out.

Then again, maybe I didn't want to know what might come out. Maybe I needed to keep whatever was in me bottled up.

With some trepidation, I found a spiral notebook

and a pen. I switched off my laptop and slipped it back in its case.

It was just me, the table, a pen, and a pad of paper.

I stared at the pen. When I grew tired of staring at the pen, I cracked my neck and my knuckles. In the hallway outside my door, I heard two voices steadily growing louder as a couple approached in the direction of my door. The couple came and went, and now their voices grew fainter and fainter.

I picked up the pen.

A domed light hung from the ceiling directly above the table. The light flickered briefly. It had never flickered before. I frowned. One of the sites I had read mentioned that when spirits were present, lights flickered.

It did so again, and again. And now the light actually flickered off, and then on. And then off. Over and over it did this.

I sat back, gasping.

"Sweet Jesus," I said.

More flickering. On and off.

Nothing else in my room was flickering. The light near the front door held strong. So did the light coming in under my front door. It was just this light, directly above me.

And then the light went apeshit. On and off so fast that I could have been having an epileptic seizure.

"Stop!" I suddenly shouted. "I get it. I'll do it."

I brought the pen over to the pad of paper, and

the flickering stopped. The light blazed on, cheerily, as if nothing had happened at all.

Okay, that settles it, I thought. *I really am going crazy.*

I set the tip of the pen lightly down on the lined paper. I closed my eyes. Centered myself, whatever that meant. I did my best to do what the article on the internet said. Imagine an invisible silver cord stretching down from each ankle all the way to the center of the earth. Then imagine the cord tied tightly to the biggest rocks I could imagine. Then imagine another such cord tied to the end of my spine, attached to another such rock in the center of the earth.

Grounding myself.

I briefly imagined these silver cords stretching down through nine hotel floors, plunging through beds and scaring the hell out of the occupants below me.

I chuckled. *Sorry folks. Just centering myself.*

When I thought I was about as centered as I could be, I realized I didn't know what to do next. Maybe I didn't have to do anything. It was called automatic writing for a reason, right?

I looked at the pen in front of me. The tip rested unmovingly on the empty page. The lights above me had quit flickering. No doubt a power surge of some sort.

Maybe I should quit thinking?

But how does one quit thinking? I didn't know, but I tried to think of nothing, and found myself thinking of everything. This was harder than it looked.

One of the articles said that focusing on breathing was a great way to unclutter thoughts. But what if someone didn't need to breathe? The article wasn't very vampire friendly.

Still, I forced myself to breathe in and out, focusing on the air as it passed over my lips and down the back of my throat. I focused on all the components that were necessary to draw air in and expel it out.

I thought of my children and the image of me strangling Danny came powerfully into my thoughts.

I shook my head and focused on breathing.

In and out. Over my lips and down my throat. Filling my lungs, and then being expelled again.

And that's when I noticed something very, very interesting. I noticed a slight twitching in my forearms.

I opened my eyes.

The twitching had turned into something more than twitching. My arm was spasming. The feeling wasn't uncomfortable, though. Almost as if I were receiving a gentle massage that somehow was stimulating my muscles. A gentle shock therapy.

I watched my arm curiously.

Interestingly, with each jerk of my muscles, the point of the pen moved as well, making small little squiggly lines on the page. Meaningless lines. Nothing more than chicken scratches.

My arm quit jerking, and I had a very, very strange sense that something had settled into it, somehow. Something had melded with my arm.

The chicken scratches stopped. Everything stopped.

There was a pause.

And then my arm tingled again and my muscles sort of jerked to life and I watched, utterly fascinated, as the pen in front of me, held by own hand, began making weird circles.

Circle after circle after circle. Big circles. Little circles. Tight, hard circles. Loose, light circles. Sloppy circles, perfect circles.

Quickly, the circles filled the entire page. When there wasn't much room left at all, my hand grew quiet.

Using my other hand, I tore out the page out, revealing a fresh one beneath.

My arm jerked immediately, tingling, and the pen wrote again, but this time not with circles.

This time words appeared. Two words, to be exact.

Hello, Samantha.

Chapter Eleven

I stared at the two words.

Had I written them? Was I deluding myself into thinking that something beyond me was writing?

At that moment, as those questions formed in my mind, the gentle shocking sensation rippled through my forearm again and the pen began moving. Three words appeared.

Does it matter?

The script was flowing. Easy to read. Big, roundish letters. Completely filling the space between the light-blue lines of the writing paper.

"You can read my mind?" I said aloud.

My hand jerked to life, and words scrawled across the page.

Thoughts are real, Samantha. More real than people realize.

I watched in amazement as the words appeared

before me. I had the sense that if I wanted to stop writing, that I could. I wasn't being forced to write. I was allowing something to write through me. If I wanted this to stop it would.

"Who are you?" I asked. My heart, which averaged about five beats a minute, had increased in tempo. It was now thumping away at maybe ten beats a minute.

There was only a slight pause, and then my hand felt compelled to write the words: *I am someone very close to you.*

"Should I be afraid?"

You should be whatever you want. But let me ask you: Do you feel afraid?

"No."

Then trust how you feel.

I took in some air, and held it for a few minutes, staring down at the pad of paper. I exhaled the air almost as an afterthought.

"This is weird," I said.

It is whatever you want it to be. It could be weird. Or it could be wildly wonderful.

Half the page was now full. My hand also moved down to the next line on its own, prompted by the gentle electrical stimulation of my arm muscles.

A weird, otherworldly sensation, for sure.

"So you are someone close to me," I said, and suddenly felt damn foolish for talking to my hand and a piece of paper. "But that doesn't tell me *who* you are."

There was a pause, and I had a strong sense that whoever I was talking to was considering how much to tell me.

For now, let's just say I am a friend. A very close friend.

"Most of my friends don't speak to me through a pen and paper," I said. "They use email or text messaging."

Words are words, are they not? Think of this as spiritual instant messaging. A SIM.

Despite myself, I laughed. Now I was certain I was going crazy.

I looked down at the printed words. The fresher ones were still wet and gleaming blue under the overhead light. The printing was not my own. It was big and flowing. My own handwriting style tended to be tight and slanted.

Finally, I said, "I don't understand what's happening here."

Do you have to understand everything, Samantha? Perhaps some things are best taken on faith. Perhaps it's a good thing to have a little mystery in the world. After all, you're a little mysterious yourself, aren't you?

I nodded but said nothing. I was suddenly having a hard time formulating words—or even thinking for that matter. I was also feeling strangely emotional. Something powerful and wonderful was going on here and I was having a hard time grasping it.

Then let's take a break, Samantha. It's okay.

We made our introductions, and that's a good start.

"But you didn't tell me your name," I blurted out.

A slight pause, a tingle, and the following words appeared:

Sephora. And I'm always here. Waiting.

Chapter Twelve

At 7:00 p.m., and still a little freaked about the automatic writing, I called my kids.

Danny picked up immediately.

"I heard about the stunt you pulled today, Sam," he said.

In the background, I heard a female voice say quietly, "What a bitch." The female probably didn't know that I could hear her. The female was now on my shit list. And if it was the female I was thinking it was—his home-wrecking secretary—then she was already on my shit list. So this put her name twice on my shit list. I don't know much about much, but being on a vampire's shit list *twice* probably wasn't a good idea.

Danny didn't bother to shush the woman or even acknowledge she had spoken. Instead, he said, "That was a very stupid thing to do, Sam."

"I just want to see my kids, Danny."

"You do get to see them, every Saturday night," he said, breathing hard. Danny had a temper. A bad temper. He never hit me, which was wise of him, because even back when I wasn't a vampire I could still kick his ass. You don't smack around a highly trained federal agent with a gun in her shoulder holster. And then he added, "But not anymore."

"What do you mean *not anymore*?" I asked.

"It means you're no longer permitted to see the kids, Sam. How can I trust you anymore after that stunt you pulled today?"

This coming from the man who had been cheating on me for months.

"Stunt? Seeing my kids is a stunt?"

"We had an agreement and you broke it, and now I have an obligation to protect *my* children."

"And they need protection from me?"

There was no hesitation. "Yes, of course. You're a monster."

I heard little Anthony say something in the background. He asked if he could talk to me on the phone. The female in the room shushed him nastily. Anthony whimpered and I nearly crushed my cell phone in my hand.

"Don't take away my Saturdays, Danny."

"I didn't take them away, Sam. You did."

I forced myself to keep calm. "When can I see them again, Danny?"

"I don't know. I'll think about it."

"I'm seeing them this Saturday."

"If you come here, Sam, then everything goes public. All the evidence. All the proof. The pathetic life that you now have will be over. And then you will never, ever see your kids. So don't fuck with me, Sam."

"I could always kill you, Danny."

"Awe, the true monster comes out. You kill me and you still lose the kids. Besides, I'm not afraid of you."

He had something up his sleeve. I wasn't sure what it was, but I suspected it was a weapon of some sort. A vampire hunting weapon, no doubt. Maybe something similar to what the vampire hunter had used on me last month. The hunter who came to kill me with a crossbow and silver-tipped arrow, and ended up on a one-way cruise ship to Hawaii. Long story.

I looked at my watch. It was well past the ten minutes he allotted me each night. "Can I please speak to my children now?"

"Sorry, Sam. Your time for tonight is up." And he hung up.

Chapter Thirteen

Fresh off my infuriating phone call with Danny, I soon found myself sitting outside Rembrandt's in Brea. I was drinking a glass of white wine. The woman sitting across from me was drinking a lemonade. Yes, a lemonade. Her name was Monica Collins and she was a mess.

We were sitting under a string of white lights next to a sort of makeshift fence that separated us from the heavily trafficked path to the 24-Hour Fitness behind us. While we drank, a steady parade of physical active types, all wearing tight black shorts, tank tops or tee shirts, streamed past our table and looked down at us gluttons with scorn. Most carried a gym bag of some sort, a water bottle, and a towel. Half had white speaker cords hanging from their ears. There was a sameness to their diversity.

This wine was hurting my stomach and so I

mostly ignored it. White wine, water and blood were the only items I could safely consume without vomiting within minutes. Wine, however, rarely settled well, but I put up with it, especially when meeting new clients. I doubted a glass of chilled hemoglobin would make them feel very comfortable.

Monica was on her second glass of lemonade. Correction, third. She raised her hand and signaled the waiter over, who promptly responded, filling her glass again with a pitcher of the sweet stuff. She looked relieved.

Monica was a bit of a mystery to me. She was a full grown woman who acted as if she was precisely fourteen years old. She had to be around thirty, certainly, but you would never guess it by the way she popped her gum, swung her legs in her seat, giggled, and drank lemonade as if it was going out of style. Her giggling was a nervous habit, I noticed, not because she actually thought anything was funny. There was also something screwy about her right eye. It didn't track with the left eye, as if it had a sort of minor delay to it. It also seemed to focus somewhere over my shoulder, as if at an imaginary pet parrot.

She had been telling me in graphic detail the many incidents in which her husband of twelve years (now ex-husband) had beaten the unholy shit out of her. I didn't say much as she spoke. Mostly I watched her...and the steady procession of humanity coming and going to the gym.

Monica spoke in a small, child-like voice. She spoke without passion and without inflection. There was no weight to her voice. No strength. Often she spoke with her head and eyes down. She had suffered great abuse, perhaps for most of her life. Women who were abused as children often found themselves in abusive relationships as adults. No surprise there.

She stopped talking when she reached the bottom of the lemonade. She next proceeded to slurp up the remnants loudly. People looked at her, and then at me. I shrugged. Monica didn't seem to care that people were looking at her, and if she didn't care, why the hell should I?

When she was done slurping, she then asked me if she could go to the bathroom.

Yes, *asked* me.

I told her that, uh, sure, that would be fine. She smiled brightly, popped her gum, and left. A few minutes later she returned...and promptly ordered another lemonade.

She went on. After she had left her husband, he had made it his life's purpose to kill her. She got a restraining order. Apparently he didn't think much of restraining orders. His first attempt to kill her occurred when she was living alone in an apartment in Anaheim.

As she paused to fish out a strawberry, I tried to wrap my brain around the thought of Monica living on her own, doing big girl things, doing adult things, and couldn't. Although thirty-something, she clearly seemed stunted and unprepared for adult life. I reflected on this as she continued her story.

He was waiting for her in her kitchen. After throwing her around a bit, he had proceeded to beat her into a bloody mess with a pipe wrench, cracking her head open, and leaving her for dead.

Except she didn't die. Doctors rebuilt her, using steel plates and pins and screws. Today she still suffered from trauma-induced seizures and had lost the use of her right eye. That explained the eye. It was, in fact, blind.

After the attack, her husband had been caught within hours. But something strange happened on the way to prison. His attorney, who had apparently been damn good, had somehow gotten him out of jail within a few weeks, convincing a judge that her ex was no longer a threat to Monica.

Her ex-husband attacked again that night.

Still recovering from the first attack, Monica had been staying with her parents when her ex-husband broke into their home, this time wielding a hammer. I was beginning to suspect someone had given the man a gift card to Home Depot. I kept my suspicions to myself.

Anyway, her ex went on to kill her father and to permanently cripple her mother. And if not for the family Rottweiler, Monica would have been dead, too. Yes, the dog survived.

Monica grew silent. In the parking lot in front of us, an older white Cadillac drove slowly by. The windows were tinted. The Caddy seemed to slow as it went by. She played with the straw. I told her I was sorry about her father. She nodded and kept playing with the straw. I waited. There was more to the story. There was a reason, after all, why she had called me this evening.

She pushed her glass aside. Apparently, she had reached her lemonade limit.

She said, "He was caught trying to hire someone to kill me."

"Who caught him?"

"The people at the prison."

"Prison officials?"

"Yes, them. But he wasn't, you know, successful." Nervous giggles.

I said, "You're scared."

She nodded; tears welled up in her eyes. "Why does he want to hurt me so much? Hasn't he done enough?"

"I'm sorry," I said.

"He's horrible," she said. "He's so mean."

As she spoke her voice grew tinier and her lower lip shook. Her hands were shaking, too, and my heart went out to this little girl in a woman's body. Why anyone would want to hurt such a harmless person, I had no clue. Maybe there was more to the story, but I doubted it. I think her assessment was right. He was just mean. Damn mean.

She spoke again, "So I talked to Detective Sherbet. He is so nice to me. He always helps me. I love him." She smiled at the thought of the good detective, a man I had grown quite fond of myself. "He told me to see you. That you were tougher than you looked, but I don't understand what he means. He said you would protect me."

I said, "In the state of California, a private investigator's license also doubles as a bodyguard license."

"So you are a bodyguard, too?" I heard awe in her voice. She smiled brightly. Tears still gleamed wetly in her eyes.

"I am," I said, perhaps a little more boastful than I had intended.

She clapped. "Do you carry a gun?"

"When I need to."

She continued smiling, but then grew somber. She looked at me closely with her good eye, not so closely with her bad eye. "I don't have money to pay you. I haven't been able to work at the bakery since he hurt me, but maybe my momma can help pay you. Detective Sherbet said that you know what the right thing to do is, but I don't know what he's talking about."

I smiled and shook my head and reached out and took her hand, feeling its warmth despite its clamminess. She flinched slightly at my own icy touch. I held her gaze, and she held mine as best as she could.

I said, "Don't worry about money, sweetie. I won't let anything happen to you, ever. You're safe now. I promise."

And that's when she started crying.

Chapter Fourteen

We were in my hotel suite.

Monica was walking around my spartan room as if it were more interesting than it really was. I sensed some of her anxiety departing. In the least, she was giggling less, which I considered a good thing.

Finally she sat on the corner of the bed, near where I was sitting in the surprisingly comfortable desk chair. My laptop was next to me, closed. Somewhere, in there, was Fang. I wondered what he was doing tonight. I wondered what he did every night. I found myself wondering a lot about him.

And what about Kingsley? I wondered about him, too, but he was a little easier to wonder about, since I knew where he lived and I knew he had the hots for me.

On the round table near me was the pad of paper that contained my conversation with...something. At least, the beginning of a conversation.

"You really live here?" asked Monica.

"For now, yes."

"And your husband just kicked you out?"

"Something like that."

She shook her head and smiled some more, but it was a nervous smile. I sensed her about to giggle, but she somehow held it in check.

"I had the opposite problem," she said.

"As in, he never wanted you to leave."

"Yes, exactly." And now she did giggle. Sigh. As she sat there on the corner of the bed, her dangling feet didn't quite touch the carpeted floor. She was so small and cute. And innocent. And sweet. And clueless. In the wrong hands, in the wrong relationship, I could see a brute of a man thinking she was his. A trophy. A little trophy. Something to possess and own. In the right hands, she would have been protected and loved and cherished.

She had found herself in the wrong hands.

Monica asked, "So why did he kick you out, if you don't mind me asking."

"I mind," I said.

She giggled, turned red, and looked away. "I'm so sorry."

I reached out and touched her knee. I had to be gentle with this one. Her social savvy wasn't quite up to par, either.

"It's okay," I said. "It's just a very fresh wound that I don't want to talk about right now. You did nothing wrong."

She nodded vigorously. I patted her knee. She looked at me, nodded again, then looked down. She was so unsure of herself. So lost. So helpless. How could anyone hurt this girl? God, I already hated her ex-husband with a fucking passion.

"Sam, can I ask you a question?"

I smiled. "Sure, sweetie."

"Can I, you know, ask how you're going to protect me?" Nervous giggle. "Is that okay to ask?"

"It's okay," I said, patting her knee reassuring, much as I would my own daughter. And the thought of my daughter—and the possibility of not seeing her or Anthony this Saturday night—nearly brought me to tears. I took a deep breath, steadied myself, and said, "You are either going to be with me, or with someone I trust. You will always be protected."

Her eyes narrowed suspiciously. She pursed her lips. "Who are your friends?"

"Good men. Honorable men. I trust them with my life. They will protect you when I'm not around."

"Why would you not be around?"

"Sometimes I have...business to attend to."

She nodded. She understood business. "And one of your friends is coming over now?"

"Yes," I said.

"Because you are going out?"

"Right. I have work to do."

"And I can't come?" She sounded like a child

asking her mother if she could go grocery shopping with her.

"Not this time," I said.

"Okay." Petulant. She didn't like the idea of me leaving her so soon. I didn't either, but what I had to do tonight she had no business seeing or being a part of.

"Chad is a good man," I said. "You will like him."

She nodded again. "Will you be back tonight?"

"Yes."

She smiled and kicked her feet out again. She was wearing white shorts. Her legs were thin and tan. They were also crisscrossed with scars. I didn't ask her about the scars, but I suspected she had been beaten badly with a belt.

"So how long will you protect me?"

"As long as it takes," I said. Mercifully, she had no children and, apparently, was on extended leave at her baking job, which I discovered was a donut shop. No wonder why Detective Sherbet liked her so much.

There was a knock on my hotel door. Three rapid knocks, a pause, and then a fourth. It was Chad, using the coded knock we had been trained to use.

"That's my ex-partner," I said. I sat forward and patted her knee again. "You're in good hands, I promise."

She smiled and popped her gum. "I believe you," she said.

Chapter Fifteen

I was sitting with Stuart Young three floors up on his balcony, overlooking a sliver of Balboa Beach. Stuart didn't quite have a water view from his balcony, but what I could see gleamed brightly under the waxing crescent moon.

Stuart offered me some wine, but my stomach was still upset from the wine I had earlier. I accepted some water instead, and now we sat together overlooking a mostly quiet street. The street ran between more condos. The condos all looked the same. Row after row, street after street, of identical condos. How I found Stuart's condo was still a mystery, especially with my dismal sense of direction.

But I knew the answer. I sensed his building, and I sensed his apartment. My psychic abilities were gathering strength.

Anyway, Stuart looked like he had recently been crying. No surprise there. He also didn't seem to care that he looked like he had been crying and made no apologies for it. His eyes were red and swollen. His nose was red and swollen. A light film of sweat coated his perfect bald head. The sweat could have been from the alcohol, since the weather is always perfect. Which is why, water view or no water view, this condo probably cost a small fortune.

Stuart was drinking light beer that he had poured into a frosted glass. Beer was the one thing I didn't miss. Blech. Give me wine any day.

"How you holding up?" I asked.

"Couldn't be worse," he said, and actually smiled.

I sipped my water and leaned slightly to the right to get a better view of the tiny sliver of ocean.

"If you look hard enough, you'll find it," said Stuart. "Believe it or not, I paid for that tiny speck of ocean you can see. Probably cost me another fifty grand."

"It's a nice speck," I said.

He chuckled and drank his beer. He seemed to be enjoying it. Go figure.

"I have it on good word," I said without looking at him, "that, unofficially, your wife's plane was sabotaged."

He stopped drinking.

I went on, "And if it was sabotaged, which appears likely, then that means your wife, along with everyone else on board, was murdered."

He sat back, stared down into his frosted mug. He didn't have much of a reaction. Then again, I wasn't telling him anything he didn't already know or suspect.

I continued, "We all know who stood to benefit from that plane going down. Jerry Blum has not only escaped prosecution, he is now a free man. With no witnesses and no case, all charges have been dropped against him."

Stuart nodded; his jawline rippled slightly.

"The plane crash investigation is still ongoing," I said after a few minutes. "The investigation could take years. Even if the authorities do find out who took it down, or sabotaged it, I suspect there will be very little evidence linking the attack to Jerry Blum."

He set his frosted glass down on the dusty, round glass table that sat between us, and turned and looked at me.

Stuart said, "And even if evidence is found indicating Jerry Blum was responsible for my wife's crash, who's to say that the next batch of witnesses won't be killed as well."

"It's a sick Catch-22," I said.

"This could go on forever."

I nodded.

"I may never see justice," he added. "Ever."

"There is still a chance they could find damning evidence linking Jerry Blum to the downed aircraft," I said.

"Or not," said Stuart.

I nodded. "Or not."

"More than likely he's going to get off, again, and meanwhile my wife...." Stuart's voice trailed off and he suddenly broke down, sobbing hard into his hands. I reached over and patted his shoulder and made sympathetic noises. He continued crying, and I continued patting.

When he finally got control of himself, he said, "I have something I want you to listen to."

Chapter Sixteen

Stuart got up and went through the sliding glass door.

He came back a moment later holding a Blackberry phone. He sat next to me again and pushed a few buttons on the phone. A moment later, the phone was ringing loudly on speaker mode. An electronic voice answered and asked Stuart if he wanted to listen to his voice mail. Stuart pressed a button. I assumed his answer was yes. The voice then asked if Stuart wanted to listen to his archive. He pressed another button, and he held the phone out between us, face up, above the round table and above his beer.

"Stu!" came a woman's frantic voice. "Stu, listen to me. Something very, very bad is happening. Oh, God! Stu, the plane is having problems. Serious problems. I heard an explosion. It happened right outside my window. On the wing. It blew up. I can see it now. Flapping, burning, on fire. This isn't happening, this isn't happening. Oh, God, Stu!" The voice stopped. From somewhere nearby, I heard a woman screaming in the background. A horrible, gut-wrenching scream. "Stu, sweet Jesus, the plane is going to crash. Everyone knows it. The pilot can't get...can't get control of it." Another pause. A voice crackled loudly over a speaker. It was the pilot. He was telling everyone to sit in their seats, to buckle up, to remain calm. And then he told them to prepare for a crash landing. "Jesus, Stu. Jesus, Jesus, Jesus. Oh, good Christ. I wish I was talking to you, baby. I need you so bad. I need your voice. Baby, I'm so scared. So scared. This isn't happening." Someone screamed bloody murder in the background. "I heard your voice, Stu. I heard it when I got your voice mail. At least I heard it one last—one more time. I love your voice, baby. I love you, baby. I love you so much. I'm going to die now." Someone spoke to her rapidly, hysterically, but the woman on the phone didn't respond. "Everyone's losing it, Stu. Everyone's freaking. Stu, the explosion. Something blew this plane up. Something blew the wing up. It's Jerry Blum, Stu. I know it. He did this, baby. Somehow. Somehow he got to us all. The motherfucker. Oh, God...." and now she broke down in sobs, briefly regained her composure, and into the phone, "I love you, baby. Forever."

And the line went dead.

***

Stuart didn't bother wiping the tears that ran down his cheeks. He stared silently down at his cell phone, which still rested in his open hand. His hand was shaking. Finally, reluctantly, he used his thumb and pressed another button, and pocketed the Blackberry carefully in his light jacket.

He said, "I forwarded my wife's message to another voice mail account I have, and then forwarded the call to the FBI. They asked me to delete the original, which I did. I never told them that I still have a copy of it. Hell, I have a few copies of it, saved in various formats. How dare they ask me to delete my wife's last message to me. The motherfuckers."

We sat quietly for a long time, and I heard his wife's panicked voice over and over again. My heart broke for her. My heart broke for him. My heart, quite frankly, broke to pieces.

"I'm so sorry," I finally said.

He nodded absently and stared off toward the beach and the muted sounds of crashing waves. I doubted Stuart's mortal ears could hear the waves. Probably a good thing, since hearing the sounds of crashing waves would have doubled the value of the condo. Just over the tiled rooftop of the condo across the street, two seagulls swooped down, their alabaster bodies clear as day to my eyes. As they flashed through the night sky, an ectoplasmic trail of crackling energy followed them like the burning tails of comets. The night was alive to my eyes. The night was alive to my ears, too.

Stuart said, "And even if the FBI eventually found the evidence to convict Jerry Blum, he still may never face punishment."

I nodded.

He shook his head. "It's...the worst feeling in the world, knowing that this motherfucker killed her, knowing that he let her burn to death." Stuart took deep breaths. "He's a fucking animal and I hate him. You know, fuck the trial. Fuck the evidence. Fuck everything. All I want is ten minutes alone with the motherfucker. Just me and him. Ten minutes."

His wishful thinking got me to thinking.

Stuart went on, "But we can't touch him. No one can touch him. Not the police, not the FBI, not the courts. No one."

"I can touch him," I said, surprised as hell that the words came out of my mouth. I really hadn't thought this through. Not in the slightest.

Stuart snapped his head around. "What did you say?"

I plowed forward, what the hell. "I said I can touch him."

Stuart squinted at me.

"What exactly does that mean, Sam?"

"It means I can hand-deliver you Jerry Blum."

"I'm not following."

It was a crazy idea. Too crazy. But Stuart was hurting and furious and frustrated, and there wasn't a damn thing he could do. Unless....

I said, "Do you really want to face Jerry Blum alone, the man who killed your wife?"

"More than life itself."

"Then what would you say if I told you that I could bring you Jerry Blum?"

"I would say you're crazy."

"Yes, maybe a little."

"But you don't sound crazy."

"Good to know."

But my crazy idea had sparked something in him. In the very least, it had given him something to take his mind off his pain. He turned in his seat and faced me.

"How could you do this?" he asked.

"I have contacts," I said vaguely.

"And your contacts can get you Jerry Blum?"

"Yes," I said. "Sooner or later."

"And I would face him?"

I nodded. "Alone."

"Man against man?"

"*Mano y mano*," I said, which, I think, meant *man and man*, but what the hell did I know?

Stuart said, "What about all his bodyguards, his shooters, his hired killers?"

I shook my head. "It would just be the two of you. Alone."

"And would anyone else know about this?"

"Just me, you, and Jerry Blum."

Something very close to a smile touched the corners of Stuart's mouth, but then he shook his head and the smile was gone. "As much as I would like to believe you, Sam, I have to face the fact that this is nothing more than a fantasy—"

"I can get him," I said, cutting him off. "Give me two weeks."

Stuart stared at me long and hard, then finally he nodded and grinned. He looked good when he grinned; it made his perfect bald head look even more perfect.

"Okay, I believe you," he said. "Why I believe you, I don't know, but I do."

We both sat back in our patio chairs and I listened to the wind and the waves and the sounds of someone in the condo below us making a late night dinner. Shortly, the smell of bacon wafted up. God, I used to love breakfast for dinner.

Stuart rolled his head in my direction. "And what if I kill him?"

"Everybody's got to die sooner or later," I said.

"You're a tough woman."

"Getting tougher by the minute," I said.

Chapter Seventeen

It was midnight, and I was sitting in my minivan with my laptop near the Ritz Carlton in Laguna Niguel. No, I don't normally hang out at the Ritz Carlton, but this was as good a place as any for what I was about to do.

Orange County's only five-star hotel sat high on a bluff, which, if you asked me, looked exactly like a cliff. Anyway, I was parked in the guest parking lot in the far corner of the far lot. I doubted I had attracted much attention. Just a small woman in a big van.

A small woman who was about to get very naked.

My windows were cracked open and far below the steep cliff—I was going with *cliff*—was the pleasant sound of the surf crashing along what I knew were mostly smooth, sandy beaches.

I briefly thought about what I had gotten myself

into, and the further away I was from Stuart and his heartbreak, the more I realized how crazy my idea had been.

Think about it, Sam: you promised to deliver one of the West Coast's most notorious gangsters to a mild-mannered widower—for a one-on-one smackdown.

Yeah, I've had better ideas.

Of course, as things presently stood, Stuart would never see justice. Or, if he did, it might be years before Blum was locked behind bars again, and that's if the feds could pin anything on him, which I seriously doubted. After all, Blum had been in prison awaiting trial when the plane went down.

A hell of an alibi.

And so what do you do, Sam? You offer to deliver a murderer to a man who's only outstanding physical attribute was perhaps the world's most perfectly bald head?

Stuart was a slight man, to say the least. Jerry Blum would no doubt kill the grieving widower with his bare hands. In fact, Blum had probably done exactly that throughout his career in crime.

And that's if you managed to somehow even get to Blum.

It's good business to under-promise and over-deliver. Well, in this case, I had over-promised...and might just very well deliver a murderer.

Great.

I shook my head. I've had better plans.

Jerry Blum needed to go down. One way or

another. Having Stuart face the gangster was probably not my best idea, but it was the best I could come up with at the time. For now, I would let the details of the showdown percolate for a few days and see what else I could come up with.

I drummed my long fingers on the steering wheel. I might be a smidgen over five feet, but God blessed me with extraordinarily long fingers. Was it wrong to really love your own fingers?

Of course, now my fingers and thumbs were capped by very strong-looking nails. Not claws, per se, just ten very thick, and slightly pointed nails. Okay, fine. They were claws. I had fucking claws.

Sometimes I hate my life.

Earlier, I had made a few phone calls to my contacts and I had gotten the address to Jerry Blum's lavish Newport Beach fortress. The gangster lived on a massive estate overlooking the ocean. In fact, it was a tiny island just off shore, but not too far offshore. A bridge connected the island.

Now, with my laptop glowing next to me, I used Google's satellite feature and studied the lay of the land from above, memorizing the various features of the island. There weren't many. The sprawling home spanned the entire north end of the island from side to side, leaving only a few acres of trees along the southern tip. For me, the trees were a good thing.

Birds get lost in trees.

But do giant vampire bats?

Once I had the images locked in my brain, I

powered down the laptop and scanned the area. All was quiet in this remote section of the Ritz Carlton parking lot. I quickly stripped out of my jeans and blouse and everything in-between. It was the in-between stuff that left me feeling especially vulnerable. And although I had been sitting in my seat for nearly a half hour, the vinyl was still cold to the touch, probably because *I* was cold to the touch, since my body heat had gone the way of the dodo bird.

Just as I got down to the bare minimum, a family of four pulled up in an SUV that was big enough to lay siege to Idaho with. I crouched low in my seat, willing myself invisible. A few minutes later, the family piled out and headed up to the hotel, and when they had disappeared from view, I cautiously stepped out of my minivan.

Naked as the day I was born.

I quickly padded across the smooth concrete, stepped over a guard rail, and worked my way through some scrubby bushes until I was standing at the edge of a very steep cliff indeed. Whoever calls these "bluffs" can bite my ass.

Up here, staring down, the ground looked impossibly far. A faint line of foaming waves crashed rhythmically against the polished beaches. I could see two people walking near the surf, holding hands. And if they should happen to look up, they might see something very, very bizarre. Something that would no doubt give them nightmares for the rest of their lives.

Then let's hope for their sake they don't look up.

I took a deep breath, filled my lungs with oxygen I really didn't need, closed my eyes, and leaped off the cliff.

Chapter Eighteen

I jumped up and out as far away from the cliff as I could.

For one brief second I was majestically airborne, face raised to the heavens, just your everyday naked soccer mom doing a swan dive off the Ritz Carlton cliffs.

The night air was alive with crackling streaks of light, flashes of energy and zigzagging flares of secret lightning. At least secret to mortal eyes.

I hovered like this briefly, suspended in mid-air, looking out over the black ocean....

And then I dropped like a rock—head first, arms held out to either side. An inverted cross.

The wind thundered over me. The face of the cliff swept past me in a blur—hundreds upon hundreds of multicolored layers of strata speeding by in a blink.

I closed my eyes, and the moment I did, a single

flame appeared at the forefront of my mind, in the spot most people call the *third eye*. The flame grew rapidly, burning impossibly bright, filling my thoughts completely, consuming my mind. And within that flame, a vague, dark image appeared. A hideous, ghastly image.

I continued to fall. Wind continued rushing over my ears, whipped my long hair behind me like a black and tattered cape. The sounds of the crashing waves grew rapidly closer. Too close. Soon, very soon, I was going to crash-land at the bottom of the cliff, splattered across the piles of massive boulders.

Would I die? I didn't know. I also didn't want to find out.

The shadowy image took on more shape, its grotesque lines sharpening. I felt an immediate and powerful pull toward the beastly image.

The image grew rapidly, consuming the flame. Ah, but it wasn't growing, was it?

No. Indeed, I was rushing toward it.

Faster and faster.

And then we were one, the beast and I.

I gasped and opened my eyes and contorted my body as great, leathery wings blossomed beneath my arms. The thick membranes instantly snapped taut like a parachute. The gravitational force on them alone should have ripped them from my body.

But they didn't rip; indeed, they held strong. My arms held strong, too.

I slowed considerably, but not enough. The boulders were still rapidly approaching, the wind screaming over my ears, blasting my face. I instinctively adjusted the angle of my arms—and now I was swooping instead of falling.

And shortly after that, I was *flying*.

I swept above the boulders, just missing them, and now I was gliding over the smooth shore, flashing over the heads of the couple walking hand in hand.

They both turned to look, but I was already gone. Just a great, black winged mystery against the starless night sky.

I flapped my great wings again and gained altitude, and I kept flapping until I was high above the dark ocean.

Chapter Nineteen

I flapped my wings again and rose another couple hundred of feet. I had about ten miles to go to get to Newport Beach. Would have taken me about twenty minutes along the winding Pacific Coast Highway. But as the crow flies, only a few minutes tops.

Or as the "giant vampire bat" flies.

I soon found myself in a fairly warm jetstream that hurled me along with little effort on my part. Far below, as I followed the curving sweep of the black coast, an array of lights shown from some of the biggest homes Orange County had to offer.

Six years ago, just after dusk, I had been out jogging along a wooded path in Hillcrest Park in Fullerton. The wooded path was one of the few such paths in Fullerton. Probably not the best time to be jogging in the woods (or what passed as woods in Orange County), but I was a highly trained federal investigator and I was packing heat.

I never saw it coming. Hell, I never even heard it coming.

One moment I was running, alert for weirdos and tree roots (in that order), and the next I found myself hurling through the air, and slamming hard against a tree trunk.

Close to blacking out, I sensed something moving swiftly behind me. I tried to reach for my gun in the fanny pack, but something was on me, something strong and terrifying.

Before my vision rapidly filled with black, I was aware of two things: One, that I was going to die tonight. And, two, the beautiful gold and ruby medallion that hung from my attacker's neck.

***

The wind swept over my perfectly aerodynamic body. A foghorn sounded from somewhere. I was unaware that the beaches of southern California had foghorns, or even fog for that matter.

I banked slightly to starboard by lowering my right arm and lifting my left. A seagull was flying just beneath me. It didn't seem to notice me, and together we continued slightly northeast, following the coast.

I had been partly correct, of course. In a way I had died that night.

Died and reborn.

And the medallion, through a series of unusual

events that I'm still not quite sure what to make of, later came into my possession. As recently as six weeks ago, in fact.

Vampires and medallions are such a cliché, I thought, as I slowly began my descent. As I did so, I recognized the glittering Newport Bay and its equally glittering pier.

Then again, maybe the vampire who attacked me invented the cliché.

Hell, maybe he was the reason for it.

***

Two joggers had found me in the woods. I learned later that the joggers had initially reported me as dead.

I awoke the next morning at St. Jude's Hospital in Fullerton, surrounded by friends and family and police investigators. Federal investigators, too, since these were my colleagues.

There had been a single ghastly wound on my neck. Whatever had attacked me had violently torn open my neck and nearly removed my trapezoid muscle.

I should have been dead.

There was no sign of sexual assault. Nothing had been stolen. Even my gun was still in my fanny pack. I was also shockingly low on blood. The only explanation that seemed to fit was that I had been attacked by a coyote, which are fairly common in those parts of northern Orange County. The loss of blood was unusual, since there had been no large quantities of it found at the scene. Again, that was attributed to the coyotes, which could have easily lapped up my hemoglobin.

And since when did coyotes prefer sucking blood to eating raw meat?

They didn't, but there was no other explanation. Yes, I reported seeing the medallion. I reported being thrown against a tree, too. These reports were largely dismissed. Sure, my detective friends joked lightheartedly about being attacked by a vampire, but the jokes were forgotten as soon as they were made.

The attack made the local papers, and there was a witch hunt on the local coyote population. Many were regrettably killed.

My neck and shoulder had required hundreds of stitches. Doctors had spent hours on it. They were expecting serious issues with infection, and I was placed in a rigid neck brace. Two days later they released me.

And that's when things started getting weird.

The morning after I was released, I noticed two things: the incessant itching under my bandages had stopped, and I was experiencing no pain in my neck at all.

With Danny watching cartoons with little Anthony, then only two years old, and Tammy at school, I went into the bathroom and shut the door and took my first look under the bandages.

And what I saw was the beginning of my new

life.

I was healed. I was impossibly healed. I was *supernaturally* healed.

I had been sitting on the edge of the bathtub with the bathroom door locked, when Danny knocked on the door and asked if everything was okay, and I said yes. But I wasn't okay. Something was wrong, horribly wrong.

He paused just outside the door, where I could clearly hear him breathing as if he was standing next to me. How could I hear him breathing from behind the door? And did I just hear him scratch himself? When he finally walked away, shuffling down the carpeted floor, I heard every step. Clearly. As if he been walking on hardwood floors.

Confused and alarmed, I crawled into the empty bathtub and hugged my knees tightly.

***

And later that day, as I nervously hid my healed wound from Danny—and alternately wondered why I was feeling a very strong need to stay away from direct sunlight—I also had my first craving for the red stuff.

What the hell was happening to me?

Chapter Twenty

From the sky, Jerry Blum's estate was easily one of the biggest for miles around. And in Newport Beach, that's saying something.

His estate was, in fact, an island all to itself, an island that was accessible via bridge from Balboa Island.

An island within an island. Cool beans.

Balboa Island wasn't a real island, though. It was just a long peninsula filled with inordinately large homes and hip bars and restaurants. I suppose calling it *Balboa Long Peninsula* just didn't quite have the same ring to it.

Still, those living on *Balboa Island* were living a lie.

Just sayin'.

Not so with Jerry Blum. He really did live on an island—an island all to himself, complete with a private bridge that arched from near the southern point of Balboa Island.

A handful of small planes buzzed around me, some beneath and some above. I doubted I was being picked up on any radar. A creature who didn't have a reflection, probably didn't return radar signals, either. And if a giant bat-like blip did show up on their radars, then that would certainly give the air traffic controllers something to chew on.

That, and nightmares.

I swept lower, tucking my arms in a little, angling down toward Jerry Blum's private island. Wind blasted me as I raced through the sky. A thin, protective film covered my eyes. Vampiric goggles.

Whoever had created this thing that I sometimes turn into had done a bang-up job. Someone, somewhere had put some serious thought into this thing.

Who that person was, I didn't know. Why I was created, I didn't know. From where this dark flying creature came from, I didn't know.

But I knew I wanted answers.

Someday, I thought.

For now, it was time to go to work.

Hey, even giant vampire bats have to make a living.

***

I found a large tree on the grounds and settled upon a thickish branch. From here, I had a good view of the rear and east side of the house.

Sometimes I wondered if I had really died that night six years ago. Maybe this was death. Maybe death was living out a nightmarish fantasy that couldn't possibly be real. Maybe death was full of wonder and fantasy.

The thick branch creaked under my considerable weight. How considerable? I didn't know, but if I had to guess, I would say that I weighed over five hundred pounds.

Big girl.

The massive estate was quiet, although men in shorts and Hawaiian shirts routinely walked the grounds. A high wall encircled the property, and barbed wire ran along the top of the wall. There were security cameras everywhere, but I didn't worry about security cameras. Two big Lincolns sat to either side of the main gate. No doubt men with guns sat in those cars. Beyond the backyard fence was the bay, and beyond that was Newport Beach itself. Wooden stairs led down from the backyard to a boat house and private pier. A sixty-foot yacht was anchored next to the boat house. The yacht looked empty, although there were a few lights on inside it here and there.

I sat unmovingly on the branch for a few more hours. My great, muscular legs never once went to sleep or needed adjusting. I suspected I could have sat perched like that all night. Or until the sun came up or until the branch snapped off. Whichever came first.

But Jerry Blum's house was quiet tonight. No

doubt he was off somewhere honing his racketeering and murder skills. Perfecting the fine art of gangstering.

I'll be back, I thought, and leaped off the branch and shot into the air.

Chapter Twenty-one

I swooped around my minivan once, twice, waiting for a security guard to move on. When he finally did, I landed softly atop the rocky cliff nearby, tucking in my wings. As usual, my wings' thick, leathery membranes hung limply, this time in the dirt. And if I wasn't careful, I could step on my wings, which I had done before and it wasn't the most graceful thing to witness. A vampire stumbling on her own wings didn't exactly grace the covers of supernatural romance novels the world over.

With the salt-infused wind hammering me atop the cliff, the flame in my mind's eye appeared again. But this time a horrific creature wasn't standing in the flame. (Unless, of course, you asked my ex-husband.) No, instead, a naked woman was standing in the flame.

A cute little curvy woman with long black hair.

It was one of the few times I actually got to see myself without heavy make-up on. Granted, it was a smallish image of myself, and perhaps only an avatar of myself, but it was me and I always loved looking at it.

And I didn't look half bad. Personally, I think Danny is crazy. Think about it, he could have had a young-looking wife for the rest of his life, a wife who never aged. Granted every decade or so we would probably have to move and make completely new friends, and he would have to put up with my cold flesh, and the fact that I drink blood, but still....

Okay, maybe I wasn't such a great prize, but I still think it's his loss.

The asshole.

And as I gazed on that image of myself, as I stood on the edge of the cliff like a living gargoyle from hell, something occurred to me, something that had been bothering me for the past month or so.

Amazingly, I still cared for Danny.

Yes, the man had made my life an absolute living nightmare. Remember, until recently we had been trying to make things work. And if he hadn't cheated on me, I would still be with him. I had planned to be with Danny for the rest of my life.

Well, the rest of *his* life.

But he had turned into his own kind of monster, which is more than ironic, and even though he began to openly cheat on me, and even though he hurt me more than I had ever been hurt in my life, I still had feelings for the bastard.

Yes, I understood why he did what he did. I get it. I'm a freak. He wanted out. But did he have to be such an asshole about things? Couldn't he have treated me with compassion and love? Did he have to act like such a douchebag all the time? Did I want to hurt him often?

The answer, of course, was yes to everything.

I sat quietly on the cliff edge, surveying the beach below. There was no one behind me, or anywhere around me for that matter. My hearing in this form was phenomenal.

Danny was the father of my children. As much as it pained me to admit it, I knew he was doing the best he could given the circumstances. How many fathers would have taken their kids from something like me? Probably many of them. How many husbands would have sought a warm body elsewhere? Probably many of them.

Yes, it would have taken an extraordinary man to get through this with me.

Danny wasn't him.

In my mind's eye, I studied the woman in the flame. She stood there passively, naked as the day she was born, watching me in return. I loved that woman. I loved her with all my heart. Life had dealt her a shitty hand, but she, too, was doing the best she could.

A moment later, I was moving toward the woman in the flame. She grew rapidly bigger, taking on much more detail. And then she was rushing at me, too, and a moment later I found myself standing on the edge of the cliff, naked, cold and crying, and staring down into the churning dark depths below, where the surf pounded rocks into sand.

Chapter Twenty-two

"I think I'm in love with her," said Chad.

It was nearly four in the morning, and we were standing just inside my hotel doorway. It had been a hell of a long night for Chad. Apparently, though, he had loved every minute of it.

"Thanks, Chad. I owe you."

"I'm not joking," he said. Chad was a tall guy, easily six-foot-three. Maybe taller. When you barely scrape five-foot-three, just about anyone looks tall as hell. Except for Tom Cruise, of course. Chad added, "There's something about her."

"She's vulnerable and cute," I said. "And you're a man. It's a simple equation."

We were whispering since Monica was asleep on my bed. We were also whispering because it was four in the morning and we were in a hotel and we weren't assholes.

He glanced over at her sleeping form. I glanced

too. Mostly under the comforter, she looked tiny and child-like. Just a little bump in a big bed. Say that five times in a row.

He said, "Sure, but there's something else." He stopped talking. Chad, I knew, wasn't used to expressing his emotions; he needed prodding, like most men. Well, those men not named Fang.

So I prodded. "You feel an overwhelming need to protect her, to help her, to save her."

Chad looked at me funny. "That's pretty much it, yeah. How did you know?"

"Because I had the same reaction," I said.

He nodded and looked back at her sleeping form. "How could anyone do that to her?"

"There are bastards out there," I said.

Chad didn't say anything at first. When Chad and I were partners we didn't talk much, but we always had a comfortable silence. When he spoke, his words weren't empty. They were full of a lot of forethought.

"I would kill him," he said. "If he ever came within a mile of her."

"That sounds like love to me," I said. "And just think, I was only gone for six hours.

"And we talked nearly the whole time."

"You mean she talked and you listened."

Chad grinned, but kept looking at her sleeping form. "Something like that."

"Get out of here and get some sleep, you love-struck puppy dog," I said. "Before you propose to her in her sleep."

"I guess I am being a little ridiculous, huh?"

I shrugged.

"This has never happened to me before," he said.

"Welcome to love-at-first-sight," I said. "Now go on."

He nodded and told me to call him anytime I needed help. I said I would and practically shooed him out of my hotel room. As I locked the door behind him, I resisted the urge to look out the peephole to see if my ex-partner was hugging and kissing the door.

With Monica sleeping nearby, I did some more work on my laptop. In particular, I got the visiting hours to Chino State Prison. On a whim, mostly because the bastard was on my mind, I headed over to my ex-husband's law firm's website. Danny was your typical ambulance chaser. He screwed insurance companies...and anyone else, for that matter.

I broadened my search on Danny Moon, chaser of ambulances extraordinaire. His name was all over the net, usually in association with some case or another, usually a case that actually went to court. You see, Danny *didn't* like to go to court. Danny was a lazy SOB, and his firm did all they could to keep cases *out* of court. But sometimes the negotiations went bad and cases actually did go to court. When they did, Danny and his firm actually had to do real legal work. Which generally made him grumpy as hell to be around.

Poor baby.

I next went to his Facebook page. I generally don't go on Facebook. It's not like I have a lot of new pictures to post, right? Anyway, I do keep an account because my daughter has one and I like to see what she's doing. Besides, Farmville is a hoot.

No, Danny and I are not friends on Facebook; apparently, divorcing someone is also grounds for dropping them as Facebook buddies. So I guess you could say I've been defaced.

Anyway, Danny kept his pictures public. Maybe he didn't know the intricacies of Facebook privacy, or maybe he didn't care.

He should have cared.

Although his pictures were very professional, everything a respectable attorney's pictures should be, there was one very *un*professional picture. Apparently Danny had been tagged at a party. And not just any party. A party at a strip joint in Riverside. And not just any party at a stripjoint, but a *Grand Opening* party.

Now, what was a respectable attorney doing at the grand opening of a cheesy strip club in Riverside?

I didn't know, but I was going to find out.

Chapter Twenty-three

It was almost sunrise and I was feeling my energy fading.

I had already warned Monica of my "condition". That is, she thought I had a rare skin disease that kept me out of the sun, which, of course, necessitated me keeping odd hours. She promised she would let me sleep during the days, and that she would not leave the hotel room on her own. I told her to wake me if she needed anything, but that I didn't awaken easily; she would have to give me one hell of a good shove, or two. I told her she could do just about anything she wanted, other than leave the suite, open the curtains, or answer the door.

She agreed to my terms, and for her sake, I hope she honors them.

My body was shutting down. Quickly. I felt vulnerable and weak and easy to subdue. But even at my weakest, I still couldn't be killed, unless someone drove a stake through my heart.

And why would anyone want to do that to such a sweet little thing?

Vampires might be immortal, but we sure as hell felt human about this time; that is, just before sunrise. (And, no, I didn't sleep in a coffin. Just give me a bed, darkness, and some peace and quiet.)

When I shut down, I do so in waves. The first, a draining of energy, always hits me about a half hour before sunrise. And ten minutes before the sun came up, the second wave hit.

That was always a rough wave. I was stuck between exhaustion and sleep. I usually lay down at this time, because within minutes I would be out cold. But when the third wave hit, I absolutely had to lie down and sleep. I was out of options.

For now I was in the middle of the second wave. The sun was minutes from rising and my body was exhausted. And that's when my IM window popped up on my laptop.

Are you up, Moon Dance?

Yes, but not for long.

First or second wave? asked Fang.

Second wave. Almost third.

So I have only a few minutes.

Yes.

I like knowing that I'm sometimes the last person you think about before going to sleep.

You've said that before.

When I was in the second wave, I was often

short and to the point and didn't feel very flirty. I felt exhausted. I felt as close to dead as a person could feel.

I also like knowing that you might dream of me.

I rarely dream, Fang. And besides, what am I supposed to dream about? Words that appear in a pop-up window?

There was a long pause. Almost too long. I felt myself going catatonic. If Fang didn't say something soon, it was going to take all my last energy to shut the computer down and crawl over to the couch in the pseudo-living room.

Then perhaps we should meet someday, Moon Dance.

Now it was my turn to pause. I sat back, and as I did so, I had the peculiar sense that something wanted to leave my body. What that something was, I wasn't sure. A part of me. Perhaps my soul, if I still had one. Within seconds I would be out cold.

Through a narrow gap in the curtain, I could see the sky lightening with the coming of the sun.

Are you being serious, Fang?

Yes.

I drummed my fingers on the wooden desk. My brain was fuzzy, thoughts scattered.

Did you say meet? I asked.

Yes. Now, sleep, Moon Dance. Goodnight, even thought it's morning.

Goodnight and good morning, Fang.

Chapter Twenty-four

"You're sure you're okay?" I asked Monica for the tenth time.

She nodded but looked a little overwhelmed. I didn't blame her. We were at Chino State Prison in Ontario, California, sitting in a stark waiting room with a few other people. I had made special arrangements with the warden for a late evening visit. Both he and the inmate agreed. Being an ex-federal agent has its advantages.

The plain waiting room was smaller than I thought it would be. We sat in plastic bucket seats that were covered with gang graffiti. Took some balls to carve gang graffiti in a prison waiting room.

Monica looked lost and fragile, and I wondered again at my logic for bringing her here. Chad was busy tonight and I had had no one else to turn to. As I was contemplating calling the private investigator

Kingsley and I had met at the beach, brainstorming out loud, Monica had volunteered to come with me, telling me she would be fine. "After all," she had said, "I'm just going to be in the waiting room, right? I won't be seeing him."

I reached out now and held her hand, forgetting for a moment that my own was ice cold. She flinched at the touch, but then gripped my hand back tightly.

"Sorry," I said. "My hands get cold."

"So do mine. Don't worry about it." She squeezed my hand again, tighter, and looked at me. "So what are you going to say to him?"

"I'm going to convince him to leave you alone."

She nodded and looked down. I didn't want to mention that maybe her ex-husband's next attempt to find someone to hurt her might slip past prison officials. Although all his calls were monitored, there is more than one way to smuggle information out of a prison.

"How are you going to convince him?" she asked.

"I don't know," I admitted. "I'm going to kind of feel my way through it."

"He'll want to kill you, too, you know."

"I'm not worried about him."

She kept holding my hand. Hers, I noticed, was shaking. I shouldn't have brought her—

But maybe this was a good thing for her. Maybe on some level, she was facing her fears.

Just then the heavy main door into the prison

opened and a young, serious-looking guy wearing a correctional uniform stepped into the room.

"Samantha Moon?" he asked.

I gave Monica's hand a final squeeze before I released it. "I'll be back," I said.

Chapter Twenty-five

Ira Lang was shown through a heavy metal door.

Monica's ex-husband was a medium-sized man in his mid-forties. He was wearing an orange prison jumpsuit, and not very well, either. The clothing hung loosely from his narrow shoulders and flapped around his ankles when he walked. He looked like a deflated pumpkin. Ira was nearly bald, although not quite. Unlike my client, Stuart, Ira did not have a perfect bald head. In fact, his was anything but. Misshapen and oddly flat, it was furrowed with deep grooves that ran from the base of his skull to his forehead. What Monica had seen in the man, I didn't know.

I watched from behind the thick Plexiglass window as Ira was led over to a chair opposite me. I noticed the guard did not remove the handcuffs, which were attached to a loose chain at Ira's waist, giving him just enough freedom of movement to pick up the red phone in front of him and bring it to his ear, which he did now. I picked up the phone on my side of the Plexiglass.

"Who the fuck are you?" he asked.

I knew the warden was listening. The warden had agreed to let me speak to Ira, anything to make this problem go away. And Ira, with his hell bent desire to kill his wife, was proving to be a huge problem for the prison.

"My name's Samantha Moon, and I'm a private investigator. I've been hired to protect your ex-wife."

"Protect her from what?"

"You."

I sometimes get psychic hits, and I got one now. I saw waves of darkness radiating from Ira. Wave after black wave. The man felt polluted. I sensed something hovering around him, something alive and something alien. I sensed this thing had its hooks in Ira. What this thing was, I didn't know. After all, it was only an impression I was getting, a feeling. Something I sensed but didn't really see. Anyway, this *something* was black and ancient and full of hate and vitriol, psychically hanging on to Ira's back, digging its supernatural claws deep within the man. I sensed that Ira had let this dark energy into his life through a lifetime of fear and hate and jealousy. And I knew, without a doubt, that whatever this thing was that had its hooks in Ira, it would never, ever let him go without a phenomenal fight. Whatever clung to Ira would cling to him until his death, and perhaps even beyond, a cancer of the worst kind.

These were all psychic hits. Impressions. Gut feelings. I get these often. Sometimes they're important, sometimes they're a waste of time. But I've learned that I should trust such feelings. And I trusted these.

A smirk touched Ira's lips. And something ancient and dark swept just behind his eyes. Whether or not Ira was possessed by something, I couldn't say for sure. But something foul and alive was eating him away from the inside out.

He asked, "So what are you, a body guard or something?"

"Or something."

He laughed, but his was a dry, raspy, dead sound. "Okay, fine, whatever. So who hired you?"

"That's none of your business."

He quit smiling and something passed behind his eyes again, a flitting shadow. Whether or not it was really there, I didn't know. And whether or not I was making it up, I didn't know, either. But there was something off about the guy. Something off, and something wrong. The moment passed and he smiled again. Amazingly, he had a hell of a smile. Perfect teeth. Okay, now I could see how he might have been engaging to a young girl fresh out of high school, which was when Monica had first met him.

"So what the fuck do you want?" he asked.

"Gee, you have such a wonderful way with

words, Ira," I said. "It's almost poetic. Maybe you should write a book of poetry in prison, rather than obsessing about your ex-wife. Call it, I don't know, *Poetry From the Pen* or, let's see, *Lock-down Limericks*."

"What the fuck are you talking about?"

"I don't know," I said. "It was a poetry/prison riff. Not my best work, but not my worst either."

He looked at his phone as if there was something wrong with it.

"Lady, either tell me what the fuck you want or get the fuck out of here."

"Okay, now there's a slap in the face for you," I said. "Dismissed by a scumbag who has nothing better to do than to play with his willy."

"Fuck off, bitch."

And as he moved to stand, I said, "Leave Monica alone, Ira."

A long shot, of course, since I suspected Ira Lang spent most of his waking hours obsessing over his wife's frustrating lack of dying. And playing with his willy.

He sat back down slowly. As he did so, he adjusted his grip on the phone, wrapping his surprisingly long fingers tightly around the receiver. His movements were all slow and deliberate, as if he had practiced them beforehand. He now placed the phone carefully against his ear and looked at me for a long, long time. I think I was supposed to be afraid. I think I was supposed to shrink away in fear. Perhaps he thought I would swallow nervously and look away. I didn't swallow, and I didn't look away. I also had the distinct feeling he was memorizing every square inch of my face.

"You want me to leave my wife alone?" he said evenly into the phone. He didn't take his eyes off me.

"Your *ex*-wife, and yes."

"Why would I do that?"

"Because I said so."

He stared at me blankly, and then laughed. A single burst of sound into the phone. He laughed again, longer this time.

"You're funny."

"When I want to be."

"You've got balls coming in here," he said. "I'll give you that much."

"The world's worst compliment to a woman."

"What?"

"Never mind. So will you leave her alone?"

He stared at me some more. I heard guards talking to each other out in the hallway. Ira and I were alone in the visiting room, since it was after hours and I had been given special access. A clock ticked behind me. Somewhere I thought I heard someone scream, but that could have just been my imagination. Or my hypersensitive hearing.

Ira cocked his head a little, and then said, "It's too late."

"Too late for what?"

"Never mind that. The bitch shouldn't have left me. I told her to never leave me."

"Gee, you're such a sweetheart, Ira. How could anyone ever leave you?"

He barely heard me. Or heard what he wanted to hear. "Exactly. I gave her everything. The ungrateful bitch never had to work a day in her life."

"People leave each other every day, Ira. It happens."

"Not to me it don't."

Ira had gotten himself worked up. I knew this because the skin along his slightly misshapen forehead had flushed a little, and he was holding the phone so tight that his knuckles looked like some weird prehistoric spine running along the back of the receiver.

Breathing harder, he said, "I will do everything within my power to make sure the bitch dies. No one leaves me. Ever."

I realized this was going nowhere fast. I honestly hadn't expected anything different, but it had been worth a shot.

"I beg to differ," I said, gathering my stuff together.

"You beg to differ what?"

"Monica very much left you, just as I'm doing now."

"I'm going to remember you, cunt."

"Lucky me."

I was about to hang up when he added, perhaps fatally, "And not just you, Samantha Moon, private investigator and bodyguard. Everyone you know and love. You have kids?"

I heard the sound of boots moving along the hallway outside. Apparently, someone listening to us had heard enough. I took in some air and closed my eyes and did all I could to control myself.

But dumbass wasn't done. He went on, saying, "I see I hit a nerve. So Samantha Moon *is* a mom."

"Did you just threaten my kids?"

"You catch on quick."

I opened my eyes and saw red. In fact, I couldn't really see at all. All I could see was a blurred image of the man behind the bulletproof glass. And I heard pounding. Loud pounding. In my skull.

The sun, I knew, had set thirty or forty minutes ago. I was at full strength. I sat forward in my chair and leaned close to the thick Plexiglass that separated us. I motioned with my index finger for Ira Lane to come closer, too. He grinned, cocky and confident, and as he leaned forward, something very dark and very twisted danced disturbingly just behind his dead eyes.

His face was inches from mine when he said, "Is there something you want to tell me, you stupid bitch? I bet you're wishing right about now you never fucked with—"

I punched the bulletproof glass as hard as I could. My hand burst through in a shower of glass and polycarbonate and whatever the hell else these things are made out of.

Bulletproof but not vampire-proof.

Ira screamed and would have fallen backward if

I hadn't grabbed him by the collar through the fist-sized hole in the thick glass. In one motion, I yanked the motherfucker out of his chair and over the counter and slammed into the clear glass barrier. His nose broke instantly, spraying blood over the glass, and two or three of his front upper teeth had broken back into his mouth. His lips were split clean through.

He flailed at my hand, struggling to free himself, but I wasn't done with him.

Not by a long shot.

Still holding him by the collar, as his warm blood spilled over the back of my hand, I proceeded to slam his face again and again into the glass, breaking more teeth, breaking his face, his skull, his cheekbones, anything and everything, and I kept smashing him into the now blood-smeared glass until I was finally tackled from behind.

Chapter Twenty-six

I nearly killed a man tonight.

Tell me about it.

And so I wrote it up for Fang, telling him everything from my first impressions of Ira Lang, to the bastard being hauled off on a stretcher. It took three huge blocks of text to get the whole story written, and when I had posted the final segment, Fang answered nearly instantly. How he could read so fast, I had no clue.

Were there any cameras in the visiting room? he asked.

No.

So there is no visual record of what you did?

Not that I'm aware of.

Don't most prisons have surveillance cameras in the visiting rooms?

Not all of them. It's up to the discretion of the warden.

So no one saw your little, ah, outburst?
No.
When you broke the bullet-resistant glass, did you leave behind any of your own blood?

That was a good question. I had cut my arm while reaching through the shattered glass. However, I hadn't bled at all, as far as I was aware. I explained that to Fang.

So you don't bleed?

Maybe, I wrote. *But apparently not from cuts along my forearm.*

Did the medical staff look at you?

They tried to, but I had wrapped my sweater around my arm, and since there wasn't any blood, they assumed, perhaps, I wasn't in need of any medical attention.

Was he in need of dire medical attention?

According to the warden, with whom I had had a long meeting after the incident, the prison doctors had determined that I had broken Ira's jaw, nose, right orbital ridge, his sinus cavity, and broken out seven teeth. He was going to need countless stitches in his mouth and hours of surgery. I related all this to Fang.

There was a long pause. I looked over at my hotel bed where Monica lay sleeping contentedly on her side. It had, of course, been a long and emotional night for her. She had visited her abusive and murderous ex-husband's prison. She had waited for me anxiously while the warden pieced together what had happened. She had been given snippets of news from the prison staff, and, she told me later, could hardly believe what she was hearing—that I had put the son-of-bitch in the hospital...even more than that, I had nearly killed him. Later that night, she sat staring at me during the entire ride home from the prison. At one point she reached out and held my hand tightly. She didn't ask me how I punched through the glass. Or how I had the strength to grab a grown man and bash his face repeatedly against the glass. She simply held my hand and stared at me, and I held hers for as long as I could before I became self-conscious of my cold flesh and gently released my grip. I saw that she was crying, but she didn't make a federal case of it. What those tears were for, I didn't know, but I suspected this had been a hell of an emotional night for her. I didn't tell her the bastard had threatened my kids. She had enough to deal with.

So what did the warden say? asked Fang.

He asked me why I didn't kill the bastard?

Was he joking?

I don't think so.

And what did you say?

I told him he should have given me another few seconds.

Jesus. What else did he ask?

He asked me how did I punch through bulletproof glass?

And what did you say?

That I was a vampire, and that if he asked me any more questions, I was going to suck his blooood. (Insert cheesy Bela Lugosi impression.)

Not funny, Moon Dance. You have put yourself at grave risk. There's going to be legal implications to this. He can press charges. There's going to be an investigation.

Maybe, I wrote.

What do you mean, maybe?

The warden heard Ira Lang threaten me.

Still, it's only a threat.

A threat from a known murderer. A threat from a man who has also been known to do anything he could to carry out such threats.

So his threat is much more than a threat.

Yes, I wrote.

So if Ira Lang did press charges, a DA may likely decide not to prosecute.

Right.

So what did you really say when he asked how you punched through the glass?

I reminded him of all those stories of mother's lifting cars off their injured children and such.

He bought that?

Probably not. He was in a state of shock himself. Everyone was.

So is that the end of the case? asked Fang.

No. Ira Lang made it perfectly clear that he wouldn't rest until his ex-wife was dead.

I could almost see Fang nodding, as he wrote: *Not to mention he could still try to carry out that threat on you and your kids.*

Exactly, I wrote.

So what's the plan? asked Fang.

If he won't rest until he's carried out violent crimes against his wife, or even me and my kids, then I think there's only one answer.

Don't tell me.

I went on anyway: *Perhaps I should hasten his rest.*

Chapter Twenty-seven

The backyard to my old house abuts a Pep Boys.

When I say *old house*, I mean my house of just over a month ago, where I had lived with my kids and husband. A house, by some weird turn of events, I had been kicked out of, even though my husband had been the one caught cheating.

Since our house sits in a cul-de-sac, we have an exceptionally large and weirdly-shaped backyard. In fact, our backyard is bigger than most little league baseball fields, which was always fun for the kids and great for parties.

On the other side of our backyard fence was the parking lot to Pep Boys, with its massive, glowing sign of Manny, Moe, and Jack in all of their homoerotic glory. I hated that sign, and thank God they shut the damn thing off at closing time.

It was well after closing time and the lights were off. *Thank God.* Manny, Moe, and Jack were sleeping. Probably spooning. My ex-partner Chad was happily watching over a sleeping Monica—at least, I hoped he let her sleep. No doubt he was watching her in more ways than one. Let's just hope he didn't creep her out too much. Chad was a great guy, even if a little love-starved.

We're all a little love-starved, I thought.

I was sitting on our backyard fence, my feet dangling down, looking out across the vast sweep of our backyard, toward where I knew my children were sleeping.

Or where they *should have* been sleeping. A flickering glow in Tammy's room meant that she was up well past her bedtime since this was a school night. Her laughter occasionally pierced the air. At least, pierced it to my ears. Actually, I could tell she was trying to laugh quietly, perhaps laughing into a pillow, but occasional bursts of laughter erupted from her.

Most remarkable, and surreal, was that my daughter was laughing at Jay Leno. I could hear his nasally laugh and wildly ranging voice—which went from high to low in the span of a few words—even from here.

Jay Leno? Seriously?

And since when did my ten-year-old daughter watch Jay Leno? And since when was Jay Leno ever laugh-out-loud funny? Perhaps a mild chuckle here and there, sure. But *ha-ha* funny?

At the far end of the house I could hear Danny's light snoring. His snoring never bothered me, since

I was a rather deep sleeper. Supernaturally deep, some might say. Anyway, mixed with his snoring was something else. Another sound. Not quite snoring. No, a sort of *wheezing* sound, as if someone was having trouble breathing through one nostril. Along with the wheezing was an occasional murmur. A *female* murmur.

My heart sank. Jesus, his new girlfriend was sleeping with him, in our bed. The fucker. Probably sleeping naked together, their limbs intertwined, touching each other intimately, lovingly. All night long.

Just a month earlier I had been sleeping in that same bed, although Danny had long ago stopped sleeping naked and had made it a point not to touch me.

The fucker.

I stared at my old bedroom window at the end of the house for a long, long time, and then I forced myself to find another sound, and soon I found it. The sound of light snoring. A boy's snore. Little Anthony was sleeping contentedly, and I found myself smiling through the tears on my face.

A small wind made its way through the Pep Boys parking lot, bringing with it the smell of old car oil, new car oil, and every other kind of oil. Living here, you get used to the smell of car oil.

I folded my hands in my lap and lowered my head and listened to the wind and my son's snoring and my daughter's innocent laughter, and I sat like that until her laughter turned into the heavy breathing of deep sleep.

I pulled out my cell phone and sent a text message: *I'm sad.*

The reply from Kingsley Fulcrum came a minute later: *Then come over.*

Okay, I wrote, and did exactly that.

Chapter Twenty-eight

I drove east on Bastanchury, winding my way through streets lined with big homes and big front yards, the best north Orange County has to offer.

It was past midnight, and the sky was clear. The six stars that somehow made their way through southern California's smog shined weakly and pathetically. The brightest one might have been Mars, or at least that's what a date once told me in college.

Probably just trying to impress me to get into my pants.

Speaking of impressing me, Kingsley Fulcrum was an honest-to-God werewolf. Or, at least, that's what he tells me.

Maybe he just wants to get into my pants, as well.

Granted, I've seen the evidence of his lycanthropy in the form of excessive hair the night *after* one of his transformations, and so I tend to believe the big oaf. But Kingsley is a good wolfie. Apparently, with each full moon, he preferred to transform in what he calls a *panic room* in the basement of his house.

Probably a good thing for the residents of posh Orange County. After all, can't have a big, bad werewolf picking off the surgically-enhanced *Desperate Housewives of Orange County* one at a time like so many slow-moving, top-heavy gazelle. Would probably hurt the ratings.

Or drastically help them; at least, until the show ran out of stars.

Stars? I thought.

Now don't be catty.

Bastanchury was always a pleasant drive, made more pleasant these days because it led to a big, beefy werewolf. I hung a left onto a long, curving, crushed seashell drive, past shrubbery that really needed to be trimmed back; that is, unless Kingsley was purposely going for the creepy feeling they invoked. Or maybe he just didn't want to make his home too inviting. I voted for both.

Soon I pulled up to a rambling estate home that sat on the far edge of north Orange County. The house was a massive Colonial revival, with flanker structures on either end, and more rooms than Kingsley knew what to do with.

I stopped in the driveway near the portico, in a pool of yellow porchlight. My minivan seemed inadequate and out-of-place parked before such an edifice. Hell, I seemed inadequate and out-of-place.

The doorbell gonged loud enough to vibrate the cement porch beneath my feet, and was answered a moment later by a very unusual-looking man. His name was Franklin and he was Kingsley's butler. Yes, *butler*. Yeah, I know, I thought those went the way of *Gone with the Wind*, too, but apparently the super affluent still had them.

Must be nice.

But in the case of Franklin, maybe not so much. There was something very off about the man. For one thing, his left ear was vastly bigger than the right. And it wasn't that it was bigger, it seemed to not, well, belong on his body at all. As if, and this is clearly a crazy thought, it had actually belonged on another person's body altogether. Perhaps strangest of all was the nasty scar that ran from under his neck all the way to the back of his head. The scar, I was sure, wrapped completely around his neck.

My instincts were telling me something very, very strange was going on here, so strange that I didn't want to believe them.

He was tall and broad shouldered, and there seemed to be great strength contained within his very formal butler attire. He looked down at me from a hawkish nose, nodded once, and asked me to follow him to the conservatory. I spared him another "Clue" game joke. This time. Next time, he may not be so lucky. Also, he spoke in what I assumed was an English accent, although it could have been Australian. I could never get the two straight. But my money was on English.

I followed his oddly loping gait to the conservatory. No, I wasn't greeted by Mrs. Plum wielding a candlestick (whatever the hell that is). Instead, I was greeted by a great beast of a man who sprung from his oversized chair with a glass of white wine in hand. How he didn't spill his wine, I didn't know. As he bounded over, exuberant as a puppy, I was half expecting him to jump up on me and lick my face clean. Good thing he didn't, since he would have crushed me. Instead, he set the wine down on an elegant couch table and gave me a crushing bear hug. I think a bone or two popped along my spine. He then led me over to the sofa where a glass of wine was already waiting for me. Along the way, he snatched his own glass.

Franklin waited discreetly near the doorway until Kingsley dismissed him. The gaunt man nodded, a gesture that was meant to be somewhat dignified; instead, it came across as sort of herky-jerky, as if the man didn't have complete control of his head.

No surprise there, I thought.

When the butler was gone, I turned to Kingsley and said, "Are you ever going to tell me Franklin's story?"

The attorney was gazing at me with heavy-lidded eyes. The air around him was suddenly charged. No, *super*charged. His brown eyes crackled with yellow fire, and he looked, for all intents and purposes, like a creature stalking me from the deep woods.

"Maybe someday," he said. His voice was thick and sort of husky.

"Was he in an accident?" I asked, suddenly a little uncomfortable. I quickly reached for the wine and sipped it, keenly aware that Kingsley was staring at me intensely.

"I'm sure parts of him were in an accident," said Kingsley. He had reached out and lifted some of my hair off my shoulder and was now stroking it delicately between his oversized thumb and forefinger.

I drank more wine, suddenly wishing like hell that I could get a serious buzz going.

"*Parts* of him?" I asked, suddenly more nervous than I had been in quite some time. "What does that mean?"

"It means...I will tell you later."

"Promise?"

"I promise."

He had slid closer to me, looming over me. I could feel his hot breath on my bare arm. I could feel his eyes on me. Crackling sexual energy radiated from him. I seemed to be caught up by it, sucked into it.

This wasn't meant to be a booty call. In fact, over the past month I had barely even kissed Kingsley. But now I felt myself curious about something more. Excited by the thought of something more. *Terrified* about something more.

But....

"I don't think I'm ready," I said, not wanting to meet his eyes. I loved those big brown eyes.

"You're trembling," he said.

"And you're breathing on me."

I saw him smile out of the corner of my eyes. He was still playing with my hair.

"How long has it been since you've had a man touch you?"

"A man? What's that? I've heard about those curious creatures."

He grinned some more. "How long has it been since you have made love, Samantha?"

"That's a little personal, isn't it?"

He laughed loudly, a sound that erupted from him with such force that I jumped. "And sharing our supernatural secrets *isn't* personal?"

"Don't use your attorney double-speak with me, Kingsley Fulcrum. I'm just not comfortable talking about it."

"Then I retract my question. I was out of line."

But he didn't stop touching my hair. Didn't stop staring at me, but I sensed that some of his supercharged energy, which had been erupting like solar flares from the sun, had died down a little. Also, his breathing wasn't so ragged, either.

I set my wine down and curled up next to him, holding his waist tightly. Kingsley reached down, wrapped a heavy arm around me and softly kissed the top of my head.

Twenty minutes later, when I felt comfortable and safe, I said, "Six years."

"Six years what?" he said groggily. I think he had been dozing lightly on the couch.

"It's been six years," I said again.

He didn't say anything at first, but I heard his heartbeat quicken. Finally, he whispered, "Too long."

I nodded and took in air I really didn't need.

Kingsley moved me aside gently and stood. His knees popped. He offered me his hand. "Come," he said. "I'm exhausted. Let's talk in bed."

"Bed?"

"Yes."

I protested some more—or tried to—but he had already snatched my hand and was pulling me through his opulent home and up his staircase, and to his bedroom and bed.

The horny bastard.

Chapter Twenty-nine

We were in bed.

I was still wearing my jeans and tee shirt. Kingsley was in a pair of black workout shorts and nothing else. We were both on top of the covers. Kingsley had his hands folded behind his head and was staring up at the ceiling. I was on my side, propping my head up with my hand, watching him. In the night, I could see him clearly. He was a little static-y; meaning, there were some limits to my night vision. Light particles flitted through the air like snow flakes caught in a car's headlights. I was used to the light particles. I barely saw them anymore.

Kingsley was a beast of a man. His body was thick and powerful and nothing like the men you see grace most muscle magazines. There wasn't a lot of definition. Meaning, he was just pure muscular mass. Maybe a few pounds overweight, but he wore the weight well. No, he wore it *perfectly*. In fact, I was certain his hulking frame would have looked emaciated if he was at his ideal weight. Tufts of hair ran down the center of his chest and spread over his flat-enough belly. I never much liked hair on men, but with Kingsley it came with the territory.

"So is that a line you use for all the girls you have over here?" I asked.

"What line?"

"'I'm getting tired, talk to me in bed'. That line."

"No," he said. "But it's a good line, apparently. I'll have to remember it."

I slapped his chest. I could have been slapping a side of beef. "Asshole."

"So, has it really been six years, Samantha?"

"Yes."

"Your choice or Danny's choice?"

"His choice, but then again, that part of me sort of shut down and never came back, either. But if he had wanted to make love to me, I would have done anything for him. What was mine, was his."

"But he didn't pursue it."

"Nope."

"Did he ever touch you again?"

"Not like that." I told Kingsley that sometimes Danny and I would get close. Sometimes we would kiss passionately. Sometimes we would be on the verge of making love, and then he would just pull back and shudder. Once or twice he vomited.

"Vomited?"

"Yes," I said. "Not something a wife wants to see after kissing her husband."

"I'm sorry."

"Me, too."

We sat quietly some more. Kingsley's eyes were open. He continued looking up at the ceiling, or at nothing. His chest reminded me of a powerful, idling truck engine.

"So, have you lost all interest in sex?"

"Well, I don't consider myself sexual," I said. "I consider myself, in fact, a monster. Monsters don't have sex."

"When was the last time you orgasmed?"

It was late. We were alone in bed. We were talking softly to each other. My innate need for privacy cringed at the question, but we were adults here, and it was a legitimate, if not too-personal question. I didn't have to answer it, but I did.

"See my comment above."

"Six years?"

I nodded. Kingsley, I knew, could see me in the dark. No doubt he saw my gesture, or sensed it.

"Hell of a long time," he said. "Do you miss it?"

"I don't think about it. Quite honestly, having orgasms is pretty far down there on my list of things to worry about. Besides, I don't think I can anymore."

"Why do you say that? Have you tried?"

I knew my face was red. A crimson-faced

vampire. Go figure. But what can I say? I never talk about my sex life. Not even with my sister, who was one of the very few who knew my supersecret identity.

"No," I said. "I haven't tried."

"You haven't *wanted to* or haven't *tried*?"

"Both. I haven't wanted to even try."

"Because you feel you are a monster. And monsters don't have sex, or orgasms, or real lives of any type."

I said nothing. What was there to say? That part of me was dead, I was sure of it.

Kingsley rolled over on his side and faced me. "You have been punishing yourself a long time, Samantha, for something that wasn't your fault."

"I'm not punishing myself," I said. "I'm dealing with it the best I know how. Besides, I don't feel sexy. I feel cold and gross, and what man would ever want to touch me?"

Kingsley suddenly put his hand on my hip as if to answer my question. His hand nearly covered my entire left hip. Jesus, he was a big boy. And then he did something that even I wasn't expecting. He gently nudged me to my back and as I fell backward, he slipped his hand between my thighs and opened my legs. His hand, through my jeans, felt remarkably hot.

I reached down and stopped him. "I'm not ready for sex," I said. "I may *never* be ready for sex."

"Who said I wanted to have sex with you?" he said, winking at me.

"Then what are you doing?"

"Just seeing how dead that part of you really is." He ran his warm palm up the inside of my thigh, over my jeans.

"I think you should stop."

"You *think*?" he said quietly, perhaps even huskily.

His hand continued up my inner thigh and I heard myself gasp. The moment I gasped Kingsley smiled again. The light particles around him were zigzagging like crazy. Like moths on crack.

"Please," I said.

"Please what?"

And then his hand lightly touched me between my legs and I reached down and grabbed his hand. I made a half-hearted effort to push it away, but his hand wouldn't move. Still, I didn't release his hand even as his thick middle finger gently stroked the fabric of my jeans. I wasn't sure if he knew what he was stroking, but the big son-of-a-bitch had found the right spot.

Lucky guess.

I gasped again and made another effort to push his hand away, but this seemed to only inspire him to work his middle finger faster.

"You deserve happiness, Samantha Moon. You are not a monster. You are a sexy woman who has been dealt a very strange hand. But I have a surprise for you."

"What?" I heard myself ask. My hands were still on his hands. It had been so long since anyone had touched me down there. So long. Hell, I had forgotten what to do with my own hands.

"That part of you *didn't* die. In fact..." And now his one hand was expertly undoing my jeans, button by button, as if he had done this hundreds of times before, which he might very well have had.

Now he slipped his hands inside my jeans, and his strong, curious fingers found their way under my panties, and now they were moving down with a mind of their own, gently parting me open.

His middle finger touched me almost hesitantly, perhaps testing my readiness. Jesus, I was ready.

And then two things happened simultaneously.

Kingsley lowered his mouth to mine, kissing me harder than I have ever been kissed in my life, and his thick middle finger slipped deep inside me.

Chapter Thirty

I had an orgasm last night, I wrote.

Good for you, Moon Dance.

My first in six years.

Must have been a hell of an orgasm.

I cried, I wrote. *I didn't think I would ever have another one.*

I am happy for you, Moon Dance. But why would you think you couldn't have one?

Because I hadn't had one in six years.

Did you try to have one?

No, not really. Danny wouldn't touch me any more, and I lost all desire to touch myself. It's hard to feel sexy or sexual when your husband finds you repulsive.

And so you touched yourself last night?

My fingers hovered over the keyboard. I knew what I was about to write next would hurt Fang. *No,*

I wrote. *I was with the werewolf.*

There was a long pause. My IM box remained static, with no indication that Fang was even typing. Finally, an icon appeared in the box showing that he was busy typing. A second later his response appeared on screen.

I am happy for you, Moon Dance. He's a lucky man.

A few months ago, after years of corresponding via chatrooms, Fang had expressed his love for me...even though we had yet to meet in person or even talk on the phone, for that matter. I wasn't sure what to think about that. I had never met anyone off the internet, let alone dated from the internet. Besides, Fang was my friend, wasn't he? He knew all the gory—and I do mean gory—details about me.

I'm sorry if that hurt your feelings, Fang.

I'm okay. Really, I am.

Well, you're a big man.

You have no idea.

Are you flirting with me, Fang?

Me? Never!

I'm not so sure about that.

There was a short pause. *I would never flirt with another man's woman.*

I snorted, although he couldn't see me snort. *And who says I'm another man's woman?*

I assumed....

You assumed incorrectly. I am still not there yet. Still not ready. I paused in my typing, thought about my words, then added: *I'm not even sure I'm close.*

Do you still think of yourself as your ex-husband's wife?

Maybe a little. I still feel connected to him. Maybe it's the kids that make me feel connected to him.

Even though he has rejected you in every way?

Well, it's only been a few months, you know. I guess I still need time to heal.

We were silent some more. Lately, I had been thinking of taking up smoking. I hadn't yet, but what the hell? It's not like I was going to ever die of lung cancer, right? Anyway, right about now I could picture myself sucking on the end of a cig just to do something with my hands. I wondered how my body would react to the nicotine.

Well, there was only one way to find out.

Fang was writing something to me, and so I waited. As I waited I looked over at Monica, who was lying on her side and reading a novel. A vampire novel, no less. Maybe I should read one of those. Maybe I could learn a thing or two.

Fang deleted his message and started over. What he deleted, I will never know. A moment later, his message appeared: *Promise me one thing, Moon Dance.*

Okay, I'll try.

Before you commit to the werewolf—or any man, for that matter—please promise me that you will meet me first.

147

But I'm not committing to anyone, Fang.

Just promise.

Okay, I will consider it. But I have to admit, I'm confused. I thought we were friends.

For a friendship to work, both people have to want the same thing. Both people have to want to be friends.

I wrote, *And if one of the friends suddenly wants something more than friendship?*

It changes things, he wrote.

I don't want things to change, Fang. I like talking to you. You are my outlet. You are my friend and my therapist and my confidant.

I want to be more, Moon Dance.

We were both silent for a long time. The hotel made typical hotel noises: a door slamming somewhere, the ding of the elevator around the corner, the endless drone of hundreds of air conditioners working hard against the warm Orange County night. On the bed nearby, Monica licked her fingers and turned the page. As she did so, her shoulder flexed a little. A narrow cord stood out on her neck. I found myself absently staring at it. Even from here, I could see it pulsating.

You there, Moon Dance?

Yes.

I want to meet you in two weeks.

I sat up suddenly. My heart, nearly useless in my chest, slammed hard once or twice against my ribs. My mouth instantly went dry. *Two weeks??* I reached for a nearby bottle of water and sipped from it, staring at Fang's words. Finally, I answered him.

Okay, I wrote. *Two weeks.*

Chapter Thirty-one

We were at our favorite bar in Fullerton, called Hero's.

I was with my sister, Mary Lou, and my client, Monica. The three of us were sitting on vinyl stools in front of a long, brass-topped bar. Our favorite mixologist was tending bar, a young guy of about thirty. The fact that he was also kind of cute contributed to the "favorite" part.

We were all sipping white wine. My sister Mary Lou was probably doing a little more than just sipping, since she was already on her third glass. It was Friday evening and the bar was hopping. This was also Casual Friday, apparently, and so Mary Lou, who worked for a small insurance agency in Placentia, was wearing jeans and a bright yellow tee shirt. For the uninitiated, Casual Friday is a sort of mini-national holiday for office workers every-where. Occurring only four times a month, Casual

Friday is commemorated by the wearing of jeans, tee shirts and sneakers, and the consumption of store-bought donuts and bagels. Homemade brownies are also acceptable. From what I understand, the day usually begins with a general air of optimism and hope, and deteriorates rapidly into a serious need to drink something strong and hard. I often reminded my older sister that every day was Casual Friday for me. And I did so now.

"Are you *trying* to depress me?" she said.

"Not clinically," I said. "But a tear or two is always nice. Besides, I have to gloat about something. There's not much else to gloat about these days."

Mary Lou didn't like her job. Unfortunately, she never did anything about it, other than bitch. My philosophy is this: Life is too short to work another minute at a job you don't love. Unless, of course, you're a vampire. And then that philosophy goes out the window.

Anyway, with my client sitting with us, my sister and I kept our conversation to mundane topics. Just three fairly cute girls, sitting in a bar, wrapped in secrets and pain and heartache.

Good times.

Mary Lou knocked back drink number three and waved the bartender over. He caught her eye, nodded, and reached under the counter for the bottle of wine. As he did so, I caught my sister adjusting her bra.

"Why are you adjusting your bra?" I asked.

"I'm not adjusting my bra," she said. "I'm adjusting my boobs."

"Happily married women don't adjust their boobs in front of cute bartenders."

"Happily married women have boobs, too," she said.

"They also have husbands."

"He's coming over—shh, quiet!"

Indeed, he was, grinning at us easily. He had short brown hair. Big brown eyes. Dimples in his cheeks and chin. He wore a combination of metal and leather bracelets, which jangled as he filled Mary Lou's glass with more wine. His sleeves were rolled up to his elbows, revealing tattoos that went down to his wrists and beyond. Some of the tats crawled along the back of his hands. His ears were pierced with silver studs, and he wore a leather strap around his neck, anchored by two huge shark teeth.

"Just a little more," said Mary Lou, slapping his hand lightly. "Pretty please."

Oh, brother, I thought, and caught Monica's eye. She smiled at me and sipped her wine, enjoying my sister's retarded attempt at flirtation. Myself, I wasn't enjoying it so much.

"If I give you more, young lady, then I have to give everyone else more," he said. "And if I give everyone else more, then my boss will fire me."

"Oh, poo. You're no fun."

He winked at me and left.

So far, Monica had remained silent and inexpressive. I sensed that her personality had been beaten out of her by her ex-husband. Sure, she had opened up to me, but not so much with other people. With that said, I suspected she didn't like my sister, either. The excessive drinking might have had something to do with it. Also, when someone laughed particularly loud, or brushed up against her, she jumped. And so she stayed close to me, like a trained puppy, never more than a foot or so away from my elbow. She felt safe with me. She *should* feel safe with me. Hell, I felt safe with me.

While we drank and talked, I stayed alert for any suspicious activity. Her ex-husband, prior to his unfortunate run-in with the bulletproof glass, had indicated that he had succeeded in hiring someone to carry out his threat on her.

Monica touched my forearm and leaned over and whispered into my ear. "I need to use the restroom."

I patted her hand. "Okay." I turned to Mary Lou. "We're going to the restroom."

Mary Lou nodded and kept her eyes on the bartender. Monica and I left and I held her hand as I threaded our way through the crowded bar. She kept about as close to me as she possibly could. Inside the surprisingly uncrowded bathroom, I waited outside the stall for her to finish her business. As I waited, I had a very bad feeling I couldn't shake. I looked over my shoulder, but we were alone. I frowned.

Shortly, we were working our way back through the bar to where we found an ashen-faced Mary Lou staring at us. We took our seats on the stools next to her, and as I sat, Mary Lou leaned over and whispered in my ear: "There was a man here."

"Who?"

She shook her head. My sister looked completely shaken. "I don't know. He came up next to me and ordered a drink."

"So?"

"He looked right at me and smiled...the most horrible smile I have ever seen."

"You're not drunk are you?"

"No, dammit." She kept shaking her head. "He looked... wrong. Off. Evil. He looked what I would imagine a killer would look like."

"A killer?"

"A hired killer."

"Is he here now?"

"No, he ordered a Red Bull, paid cash, and left. Right before you two came back. He wanted me to see him. He wanted you to know he's watching."

"And you're not drunk."

"Goddammit, no."

My first instinct was to run out after the guy. Maybe that's what he wanted me to do. Maybe. The sun was still an hour or so from setting. I wasn't at my strongest, and I wasn't going to leave Monica.

"Okay," I said to Mary Lou. "Hang on."

I motioned for the bartender. He saw me immediately and, even though he was talking to someone else, said something to them, laughed, and came right over. He looked curiously at my mostly full drink.

"You need something else?" he asked.

I nodded. "The guy who ordered the Red Bull a minute ago. Have you ever seen him in here before?"

He shook his head. "No. Why?"

"How tall would you say he was?"

He shrugged. "Six foot maybe. Why?"

"How old would you say he was?"

He shrugged again. "Hard to say. Forty, fifty. Is everything okay?"

"We'll see," I said. "Can you tell me any more about him?" I wanted a description of the guy from someone who wasn't nearly three sheets to the wind.

The bartender studied me with his big brown eyes. His shark teeth glistened whitely at his throat. He had been working here for a few months, but he had never really spoken. Still, I often caught him catching my eye. I think he thought I was cute. Go figure. Finally, he said, "White guy. Thin. Black hair. Black eyes. Probably brown eyes, but they looked black in here."

"Anything else about him?" I asked.

"He was wearing a sign around his neck that said, 'I am exhibiting suspicious behavior.' Does that help?"

"I don't tip you to be funny," I said.

"The humor is free."

I looked away from him, scanning the room. I didn't sense any immediate danger. The sensing of danger is tricky business for me. Lots of things set off my warning bells. If the man honestly didn't intend any sort of physical violence at this moment, I probably wouldn't have picked up on anything. Now, had he been charging us with a pocket knife at this very moment, my spidey-senses would have sprung to life.

I turned back to the bartender, who was watching me curiously. "So that's all you remember?"

He grinned easily. "Hey, he just ordered a Red Bull to go. I think I did pretty good remembering what I remembered."

"Bravo. You get a biscuit."

"So what's this all about anyway?"

"Official undercover chick business," I said.

He nodded. "I see. Well, be safe under those covers, young lady," he said, and then moved quickly away to get another drink order filled.

I turned to Monica; she was staring at me, having heard everything of course. "Is he a bad man?" she asked.

"I don't know," I said.

"Does he want to kill me, too?"

"I don't know," I said, frowning. "But no one is going to kill you or hurt you or anything. I promise."

She smiled, or tried to, and gripped my arm even tighter.

Chapter Thirty-two

I called right at 7:00 p.m.

Danny picked up and told me to hold on. No other pleasantries were said. There were never any pleasantries said. While I waited and while I listened to him breathing steadily on his end, I thought of us standing together in the shade of the Fullerton Arboretum. It had been a small wedding. Just forty or so family and friends. It had been a beautiful, sunny day. Danny had looked so handsome and awkward in his suit. He kept folding his hands over and over at his waist, trying to look dignified standing in front of everyone, but mostly looking nervous as hell. I had watched him the entire way as walked down the aisle with my father. Danny had watched me, too, and the closer I got the more his nerves abated. He quit fumbling with his hands. He then smiled at me brighter than he had ever smiled at me before or after.

I heard something akin to a hand covering the phone, heard muffled voices, then more scraping sounds and Danny spoke into the phone. "You've got eight minutes."

"Eight!?"

A second later, a squeaky little voice burst from the line.

"Mom!"

"Hi, baby!"

"Don't call me baby, mom. I'm not a baby."

"I'm sorry, Mr. Man."

"I'm not a man, either."

"Then what are you?"

"I'm a boy."

"You're my big boy."

He liked that. I could almost see him jumping up and down on the other end of the line, pressing the phone into his ear with both hands, the way he usually does.

"Daddy says you can't come see us tomorrow. That you are too busy to see us."

"That's not true—"

"Yes, it is true, Sam," said Danny's voice. He had, of course, been listening in from the other phone, as he always does. "You're busy with work and you can't see them."

I took in a lot of air, held it. Let it out slowly.

"I'm sorry, angel," I said to my boy. "I'm going to be busy tomorrow."

"But we never get to see you—"

"That's enough, Anthony. Get your sister on the

line."

A moment later, I heard Tammy say, "Give me that, jerk," followed by Anthony bursting into tears. Sounds of running feet and crying faded quickly into the distance, followed by a door slamming. He was probably crying now into his pillow.

"Hi, mommy," she said.

I was too broken up to speak at first. "Is Anthony okay?" I asked, controlling my tears.

"He's just being a baby."

"No, he's just being a little boy."

"Whatever," she said.

"Don't 'whatever' me, young lady."

She said nothing. I heard the pop of chewing gum. I also heard Danny making tiny shuffling movements on his end of the line. No doubt looking at his stopwatch. Yes, stopwatch.

"What did you guys do today?" I asked.

"Nothing," she said.

"How was school?"

"Boring."

"Did you do your homework?"

"Maybe."

"Is that a yes or a no, young lady?"

"It's a *maybe*."

I knew Danny was on the other phone, listening, hearing his daughter disrespect her mother, and not giving a damn. I let the homework go. She was right, after all. I presently had no say in whether or not the homework got done, nor did I have any way of enforcing any house rules. I knew it. She knew it.

I also suspected she was deliberately hurting me, since my unexplained absence was hurting her.

"I miss you," I said. "More than you know."

"You have a funny way of showing it, mom."

"I'll figure out a way of seeing you guys more soon. I promise."

"Whoopee."

"That was rude," I said.

"So?"

"Don't be rude to your mother."

"Whatever."

I took a deep breath. I knew my time was running out fast. I suspected Danny sometimes cut our conversations short. Either that, or time disappeared when I spoke to my kids. Even when they were being impossible.

I said, "I promise, I'll see you as soon as I can."

"Tomorrow?" she asked, and I heard the faint hope in her voice. She was still trying for badass pissy, but the little girl who missed her mother was still in there.

"Not tomorrow, angel," I said, my voice breaking up. "But soon."

She was about to say something, probably something mean or rude or both. But something else came out entirely. A small, hiccuppy gasp. She was crying.

"I love you," I said. "I love you more than you could possibly know."

"I love you, too, mommy," and then she really started crying, and I was crying, and Danny stepped in.

"Time," he said.

"Goodbye, angel," I said quickly. "I love you!"

She was about to say something when the line went dead.

Chapter Thirty-three

Monica and I were sitting in my minivan down the street from my house. Very far down the street. In fact, we were at the *opposite end* of the street. Still, from here I could see my house—yes, *my* house. In particular, I could see anyone coming or going, especially Danny and his lame new Mustang.

Mustang? Weren't those for college girls?

Also from here, I could see the Pep Boys' sign rising above the house. Looming, might be a better word. The lights in the sign were currently out. The boys were asleep. Allegedly.

The night was young and some in the neighborhood were still out and about: pushing baby strollers, walking dogs, jogging, or, in one case, power walking.

My windows were heavily tinted for two reasons: The first was because I happened to be fairly sensitive to the sun. Go figure. The second was because I often used my nondescript minivan for surveillance. And when I was doing a lengthy surveillance, I would actually pull down a dark curtain from behind the front seat and hunker down in the back of the van, looking out through the many blackened windows. I even had a port-a-potty for long surveillances.

Tonight I didn't expect to need my port-a-potty. Tonight I expected the action to begin fairly quick. Call it a hunch.

"So is this a real stakeout?" asked Monica. She was sitting cross-legged in the passenger seat. She could have been a teenager sitting there next to me.

"Real enough," I said.

"And that's your old house up there?"

"Yes."

"So are we stalking your ex-husband?"

"I'm a licensed private investigator," I said. "I'm licensed to stalk."

"Really?"

"In most cases."

"What about this case?"

"In this case," I said. "We're stalking the hell out of him."

She giggled. If Danny spotted me following him, he could report me to the California Bureau of Investigative Services, where I would probably be heavily fined and face jail time, probably a year. The CBIS frowned upon investigators abusing their privileges.

Which was why I was parked *way down* the
street. Back when I had first caught Danny cheating
on me, I had been reckless and he had spotted me.

This time, I intended to play it safe.

"So what's it like having kids?" asked Monica.
She was chewing some gum, occasionally popping
bubbles inside her mouth, the way kids used to do it
back when I was in high school. I never did figure
out how they did that, or how she was doing it now,
and with that thought, something fairly exciting
occurred to me.

Hey, I can chew gum!

At least gum that had no sugars in it at all. I
asked Monica for a piece and she reached into her
little purse and produced a rectangular square. It
was cinnamon and sugar free. I had no clue what it
would do to me, but I was eager to find out.

God, I'm pathetic.

I unwrapped the gum hastily and tossed the
discarded paper in my ash tray. Saliva filled my
mouth as the sharp bite of cinnamon tore through
even my dulled taste buds. Cautiously, I swallowed
my own saliva, now filled with cinnamon flavor.

I kept an eye on my dashboard clock. I would
know in less than two minutes if my body would
reject even this small amount of flavoring.

And while I waited, I chewed and chewed,
savoring the flavor, savoring the smooth texture of
the gum on my tongue and in my mouth. And, like
riding a bike, I produced my first bubble in six
years. It popped loudly and Monica giggled. And

just as I was scraping the gum off my nose and chin, something in my stomach lurched.

But that's all it did.

Lurched.

Nothing came up. No extreme pain. Nothing more than that initial, slightly painful gurgle. I grinned and continued happily chewing the gum.

So there you have it. Vampires can chew gum. Wrigley should consider a new slogan: "So good, even a vampire won't projectile vomit."

I asked Monica for the brand name of the gum, and she fished the package out again and told me. I grinned. Hell, I was going to buy stock in the company.

"Look," said Monica pointing through the windshield excitedly. "Someone's leaving your house."

I took my binoculars out and adjusted them on the medium-sized figure. It was Danny, and he was dressed to kill.

Chapter Thirty-four

In his girly Mustang, he exited the driveway, drove briefly towards us, and then hung a left down a side road inside the housing track. I started the van and pulled slowly away from the curb. Like a good girl, Monica checked her seat belt. She was grinning from ear to ear. I'll admit, P.I. work can be fun.

Twenty seconds later, I made a right onto the same road Danny had made a left onto. As I did so I caught a glimpse of him making a left out of the track, and onto Commonwealth Avenue.

It was just past ten and I wondered who was watching the kids. Until I realized it was, of course, his slutty, ho-bag secretary.

I gripped the steering wheel a little tighter.

You probably don't want to piss-off a vampire. Just sayin'.

Anyway, I hung a left on Commonwealth, and easily picked up the shape of the Mustang's taillights about a half mile down the road. One thing about my current condition, my eyesight was eagle-like. And it only got better when I was in my, well, eagle-like form. Or bat-like. Or whatever the hell I transformed into.

While tailing someone, I could hang back farther than most investigators could. Still, it was a fine balance of staying far enough back to not get spotted, but not so far that I hit a red light and lost him altogether. I should probably have rented a car for tonight, but it was too late now.

Live and learn.

Next to me, rocking slightly in her seat, Monica was chewing her nails nervously. From my peripheral vision, her mannerisms and sitting position suggested she was no older than ten years old. About the age of my daughter.

My cell rang.

Shit. I dreaded looking down. Was it Danny? Had he spotted me already? Impossible.

It continued ringing and finally I reached for it in the center console, where it had been charging. I looked at the faceplate. It was Kingsley.

I unhooked the phone from the charging wire.

"Arooo!" I sang, "Werewolves of London...."

"Not funny," he said, his deep voice rumbling through my ear piece. "And please not over the phone."

"Big brother and all that," I said.

"Something like that."

"You sound like you're in a pissy mood," I said.

"I am." He paused on the other end. Up ahead, Danny took a right onto Harbor Boulevard. He didn't use his blinker. I should make a citizen's arrest. Kingsley went on, "You nearly killed my client the other day."

I turned onto Harbor as well. I wasn't sure I heard Kingsley right. "Your client? What do you mean?"

"Ira Lang."

I nearly dropped the phone. "Excuse me?"

"Ira Lang is my client, Samantha. And he's been my client for the past few years, since his first arrest. Now he's in the hospital, with a face full of metal pins and screws and staples."

I looked over at Monica, who was still peering ahead, rocking slightly. From this angle, I could see where her left eye drooped badly, the result of her husband's attack with a hammer, the attack which had resulted in Ira's first arrest.

Kingsley's words had sucked the oxygen from my lungs. I found myself driving on automatic, vaguely aware that I was still following the Mustang far ahead. Danny was slowing for a red light. There were three cars between us, and he was still a quarter mile down the road.

"This is a problem," I said.

"Damn straight, Sam. My client's going to press charges."

"I'm not worried about that," I said. "Let's talk

later, Kingsley. This isn't a good time."

"Swing by my place when you get a chance."

"Okay," I said, and hung up.

Monica was watching me curiously. She, like most people, was far more psychic than she realized. She had picked up something in my voice, something in my mannerisms. She knew something was wrong.

Hell, yeah, something was wrong. The guy I was seeing—the guy who had touched me more intimately than any man had touched me in a long, long time—had gotten her ex-husband out of jail on a technicality.

Who then went on to bludgeon her father to death.

Sweet Jesus.

Monica was still watching me. I looked over at her and gave her the brightest smile I could muster. It seemed to work. She smiled back at me sweetly, reminding me of a child all over again, a child eager for good news.

I reached out and held her hand; she held mine in return, tightly. I continued following Danny at a distance, and holding Monica's hand.

Chapter Thirty-five

We were sitting outside a strip club. A filthy, disgusting, vomitous, vile strip club.

We had followed Danny down the 57 Freeway, and then east along the 91 Freeway. He had gotten off in the city of Colton, a tough little area in Riverside County. We were about 60 miles east of Orange County. Here, they did not make reality shows about super-enhanced married women. Here, there was crime and gangs and a sense that something, somewhere had gone very wrong with this city. So wrong that it was beyond hope to fix.

Danny had worked his shiny Mustang along the dark and dirty streets, far removed from our cute little neighborhood, and had ended up at a small strip joint at the far edge of the city.

By the time we had pulled up to the club, Danny was already inside. I circled the packed parking lot, found his car, and then parked as far away from it as I could, all while keeping an eye on the club's front door.

We parked and cracked our windows. Music thumped through the club's open door. Two rather large black men stood on either side of the door. In a raised truck about five cars away, I was pretty sure two people were having sex. Already I felt I needed to shower.

Monica had seemingly shrunk in on herself. She pulled her feet up on the passenger seat and wrapped her arms tightly around her knees.

I was, admittedly, confused as hell. I had never known Danny to be the type to go to strip clubs. Of course, I had never known Danny to be a cheater and a liar and royal piece of shit, either, until recently.

I was tempted to look inside the club, but I wasn't going to bring Monica with me, and I sure as hell wasn't leaving her alone.

And so we sat, staring at the entrance to the strip club. Amazingly, I still felt a pang of jealousy that Danny would find pleasure in looking at other women. That is, until I reminded myself that he had been sleeping with another woman for the past few months.

I felt sick. I felt disgusted. I felt a massive wave of revulsion.

Monica was rocking now. The thumping music and the trashy cars and the trashy guys were all too much for her. She reminded me of a child sitting in her bedroom and listening to her parents fighting downstairs. Listening and rocking and suffering.

I waited another half hour, watching Monica, watching the door, watching the waves of men coming and going. Danny remained inside.

I was having a hard time believing Danny had come all this way to a strip club. There were clubs a lot closer than this. Not as sleazy, certainly, but a lot closer. So why had Danny driven nearly an hour to go to this shit hole? I didn't know, but I was going to find out.

I started the car and left.

Monica rocked in her seat nearly the entire way home.

Chapter Thirty-six

I comforted Monica with hugs and hot tea.

When she seemed stable again, I called my ex-partner. He was more than up to the challenge of watching over Monica again. In fact, I suspected he might have been waiting eagerly by his phone, since he had snatched it up on the first ring.

Thirty minutes later, with Monica in good (if not adoring) hands, I made my way over to Kingsley's massive estate. Franklin the Butler did not seem pleased to see me this late, and I once again followed his slightly off-kilter, loping gait. This time to the kitchen, where I found Kingsley sitting at a round corner table, working on a double-stuffed ham sandwich. Sitting across from him was a glass of red wine. Mine, I assumed, although I rarely drank red wine since it gave me stomach cramps. Too many impurities.

Kingsley thanked the butler, who expressed his love of servitude with words dripping with sarcasm, and disappeared down a side hallway. To where, I had no clue. No doubt a servant's quarter.

Or perhaps a stone slab with straps and thick cables attached to some sort of medieval antennae on the roof.

Or not.

As I stepped into the kitchen, Kingsley set aside the heavy-looking sandwich and got up and gave me a hug and a light kiss on the lips. The light kiss was my idea. I turned my head, since I wasn't in much of a kissing mood. Kingsley indicated the chair across from him, and as I sat, I realized the glass wasn't full of wine, it was full of something else.

It was full of blood.

Saliva burst instantly from under my tongue. I might have even licked my lips. *Might have.*

Kingsley was watching me. "You don't have fangs."

"What an odd thing to say to a girl," I said, keeping my eyes on the hemoglobin-filled goblet. Say that three times in a row.

"I noticed it the other night, in bed, when we were kissing. Your teeth are normal."

"Gee, thanks."

"But I thought vampires had fangs," he pushed.

"And I thought vampires existed only in teen romance novels."

He chuckled lightly and let it go. I noticed the

blood in the goblet was beginning to congeal a little along the surface, sticking to the inside of the thick glass. It was just blood. Disgusting blood. But it was the only thing I could consume comfortably. It was the only thing that gave me nourishment. And now, over the course of six years, blood had become my comfort food. Hell, it had become my only food, My everything. My stomach was doing back flips.

God, I was such a fucking ghoul.

"Drink, honey," he said. As he spoke, he used some strange German accent. Oh?

"Who's blood is it?" I asked.

"Does it matter?" His voice was back to normal.

He was right, of course. I had discovered that the source of the blood mattered not at all. Human, animal, warm, cold. It all had the same effect on me: it nourished me deeply.

I picked up the glass and drank deeply. The blood was warm. It was fresh, too. Something had recently died. Blood has a unique texture and I have grown to both love and loathe it. Good blood, fresh blood, is heavenly. The blood I normally drank, blood provided to me from a local butchery, was filled with all sorts of disgusting "extras", which I constantly found myself spitting out.

Yum.

My account with the butchery was more or less a secret account. The butchery was in Chino Hills, and six years ago, I had convinced the owner I was a vet assistant and that I was involved with animal blood research. He hadn't asked questions, and I hadn't provided any more info other than that. The blood arrived monthly and I paid the exorbitant bill. Meals on wheels.

With that said, this blood was flawless, minus one or two coagulated lumps. I drank from the goblet steadily, briefly unable to pull away from it. Salty and metallic, it coated the inside of my mouth, filling the spaces between my teeth. I didn't need to come up for air because I really didn't breathe.

I drank steadily, greedily, happily.

When the goblet had been half-drained, I forced myself to set it down in front of me, and burped.

"Hungry?" asked Kingsley.

"Usually," I said.

"So how often do you eat?" asked Kingsley, and I silently thanked him for not using the word "feed". The word rubbed me the wrong way. Animals *feed*. Monsters *feed*. Ladies with degrees in criminal justice, who had two wonderful children and a successful private eye firm didn't *feed*. We drank, even if our food was liquified.

A smoothie from hell.

"I'm hungry every night," I said, shrugging. "Like most people."

"Most people eat during the day."

"You know what I mean," I said, picking up the glass again. "Asshole."

He grinned. "Do you eat every day?"

"No."

"Why not?"

"Because the packets of animal blood disgust me."

"I've seen your packets," he said, shuddering. "Revolting." He looked at me some more, his sandwich looking miniscule in his oversized hands. "So, then, is it safe to say that you go as long as you can without eating?"

"Yes."

"And how long can you go without eating?"

"Three or four days."

"And then you have to eat."

I nodded, tilting the glass up to my lips, reveling in the purity of the blood, letting it coat my tongue, the roof of my mouth.

"Do you ever worry that you will go too long between meals, and find yourself so hungry that you might do something stupid?"

"Like kill someone?" I asked.

"That would be something stupid, yes."

"I'm not worried," I said. "Not really. I'm generally always close to a source of blood. When I'm hungry enough, I just pop open a packet."

"There might come a day when you don't have such a ready source of blood."

"Maybe," I said. "But I'll cross that bridge when I come to it."

And with that, I finished the glass of blood. I brought it over to the sink and immediately washed it out. When I wasn't hungry, the sight of blood made me want to vomit.

About that time, Kingsley stuffed the rest of his

sandwich in his mouth, chewed a half dozen times —surely not enough to fully masticate such a large section of sandwich—and then swallowed it down like a whooping crane, tossing back his head.

We both sat back, looking at each other.

"We have a problem," I said.

Kingsley nodded. "Is it that I'm too sexy?"

I didn't feel like smiling. I felt like clawing his eyes out, if you wanted to know the truth. "You got Ira Lang out of jail the first time around," I said.

"Sure," said Kingsley, shrugging. "And he didn't even have to pay me."

"What do you mean?"

"I was his court-appointed attorney."

"But I thought you were one of the most expensive defense attorneys around."

"I am. But sometimes when there are emergencies or the other attorneys are swamped, a judge will ask me to take over a case."

"So you took over the case."

He winked. "Of course. You don't say no to a judge."

"But Ira tried to kill his wife," I said. "And not just *tried*. The piece of shit did everything within his power to kill her."

"Right. And I got him out of jail," said Kingsley evenly. "It's what I do best."

I searched for words, fought to control myself.

As I did so, Kingsley continued, "Look, Sam. Don't take this so personally, okay? If it wasn't me getting him out of jail, any other defense attorney worth his salt would have done the same. Ira had no previous record. He was a first time offender. He was ordered to stay away from his wife—"

"And I am sure you are proud of yourself for getting him out."

"I did my job well."

"And how did you feel when you heard the news that he had gone after her again, but this time killing her father, who fought to protect her?"

"It was unfortunate."

"And you couldn't have seen that coming?"

"I saw it coming."

"But you did nothing to stop it."

"It's not my job to stop it, Sam. It was my job to get him out of jail."

"You're an animal," I said.

He folded his arms over his great chest. His black tee shirt was stretched to the max over his biceps and shoulders and pectorals and even his slightly-too-big gut. His deep voice remained calm; he never once took his eyes off me.

He said, "You are emotional because you have grown close to the victim."

"I am emotional because I let an animal put his hands on me."

"I seem to recall that you liked my hands on you."

I stood abruptly. "I can't talk to you right now."

He stood, too, and grabbed hold of both my shoulders. He towered over me. His shaggy black hair hung down over over his face. He smelled of pastrami and good cologne. He had put the cologne on for me, I realized. He had wanted more tonight, perhaps to sleep with me. I shuddered at the thought.

"Don't go," he said. "I'm not the enemy."

"No," I said. "But you might as well be."

He tightened his grip on my shoulders, but with one swipe of my hand, I easily knocked them off. Shaking, I turned and walked out of the kitchen.

"Don't go," he said after me.

I didn't look back.

Chapter Thirty-seven

I sat on the same thick tree branch and watched the crime lord's regal estate. Just a giant black raptor with a love for cute shoes.

The massive island home was ablaze with lights as Jerry Blum did his personal best to accelerate global warming. Activity had picked up since the last time I was here a few days ago. Now there were more guys with big guns, more beautiful women, and more cars coming and going. The cars looked armor plated. Once, a man and a woman strolled beneath the very tree I was perched in. The man lit a cigarette. The woman was wearing a blouse cut so low that I could see straight down it to her belly button. Probably a good thing neither of them thought to look up.

As I watched them, sitting motionless and squatting on the thick branch, I wondered if I emitted an odor of some sort. I had read years ago that Bigfoot sightings were often preceded first by a horrific stench. Well, I had showered just a few hours earlier, thank you very much. Granted, I had showered as a *human*. Either way, neither crinkled their noses and looked at each other and asked, "Do you smell a giant vampire bat?"

Again, probably a good thing.

The man finished his cigarette and mentioned something about being off in a few hours and why didn't she come up to his room then? She said sure.

He nodded and flicked his cigarette away, and Mr. Romantic and Slutty McSlutbag drifted off over the grounds, to disappear in the controlled mayhem of the estate house. Something seemed to be up, but I didn't know what. I caught snatches of conversation, but couldn't piece anything together. Once I saw Jerry Blum himself, surrounded by a large entourage of men. Big men. Dark-haired men. They moved purposely through the house, and I watched them going from window to window, until they slipped deeper into the house and out of view.

Jerry was going to be hard to get alone. But I was a patient hulking monster.

As the wind picked up and the tree swayed slightly, I adjusted my clawed feet, stretched my wings a little, and hunkered down for the night.

Chapter Thirty-eight

I turned off Carbon Canyon Road, which wound through the Chino foothills, and onto a barely noticeable service road.

Stuart Young, my beautifully bald client who was sitting in the passenger seat next to me, looked over at me nervously. I grinned and winked at him.

"Um, you sure you know where you're going?" he asked.

"No clue," I said.

"Of course not," he said good-naturedly. "Why should you? We're only driving through the deep dark forest in the dark of night."

"Fun, isn't it?"

I doubted we would get lost since there was only about a quarter mile of wilderness between the road and the grass-covered hill before us. Even a soccer mom could get her bearings here. We had been driving down the twisty Carbon Canyon Road, a road some think of as a sort of shortcut from Orange County to Riverside County, but, if you ask me, it's just a more scenic way to fight even more dense traffic.

The van probably wasn't made for dirt roads, but it handled this one well enough. We bounced and scraped through shrubbery until we came across a metal gate that consisted of two horizontal poles.

"It looks locked," said Stuart.

"Hang on," I said.

I put the van in park and hopped out, brushing aside a thorn covered branch with my bare hand. A thorn or two snagged my skin and drew blood. By the time I reached the gate, my hand was already healed.

Cool beans.

A thick chain was wrapped around a rusted pole driven deep into the ground. The chain was padlocked with a heavy-duty lock. I often wondered who carried keys to these random city and county locks. Somewhere out there was a guy standing in front of some obscure park gate with a big wad of keys and going crazy.

This lock was a big one, and heavy, too. As I picked it up, the chain clanked around it. I turned my back to Stuart. I hooked my finger inside the lock's rusted loop and with one quick yank, I snapped the lock open.

"We're in luck," I yelled, letting the lock drop. "It's open."

***

We were now in a clearing at the edge of a ravine, where a small river flowed twenty feet below. The gurgling sound of it was pleasant. The chirping of the birds was even more pleasant. Darkness was settling over what passed as woods in southern California, which amounted to a small grove of scraggly elderberry trees, deformed evergreens, beavertail cactus, and thick clumps of sagebrush and gooseberry, and other stuff that wasn't taught in my junior college environmental biology course.

We were in a sort of clearing, surrounded by a wall of trees. My sixth sense told me that this place had been used before, for something else, for something physically painful, but I didn't know what. My sixth sense was sketchy at best. Still, I heard the crack of something breaking, perhaps bone, and I heard the crash of a car. I walked over to the edge of the ravine and looked down. Sure enough, deep within the soft soil around the lip, I saw deep tire tracks. Someone, at sometime, had taken a nose-dive off the edge here and down into the river below.

I turned and faced Stuart. "This is where I will bring him."

Stuart had walked to the center of the clearing, and was taking in the area, perhaps envisioning himself fighting a crime lord to the death in this very spot. Like gladiators in an arena.

"It's a good place," he said, nodding. He looked slightly sick.

A bluejay shot through the clearing, flashing through the shadows and half light, disappearing in the branch high overhead, reminding me of the old George Harrison song, "Blue Jay Way", about fogs and L.A. and friends who had lost their way.

I stood in the clearing with a man who had lost his way, too, his life completely derailed by pain and grief and the burning need for revenge. He stared up into the darkening sky, which filled the scattered spaces above the tangle of trees. His bald head gleamed dully in the muted light.

We all lose our way, I thought. *Some of us just for longer than others.*

Perhaps even for all eternity.

"A part of me doesn't believe you can get him here," said Stuart, still looking up, his voice carrying up to the highest, twisted branches.

I said nothing.

"But another part of me believes you can. It's a small part, granted, but it believes that you can somehow, someway, deliver Orange County's biggest son-of-a-bitch to me."

I was quiet, leaning my hip on the fender of the minivan, my hands folded under my chest. A small, hot wind blew through the clearing.

"So then I ask myself, 'What will you do if he does show up? What will you do if Samantha Moon really can deliver him?'" He lowered his head and looked over at me, his face partially hidden in shadows. I could mostly see through shadows, but I doubted he could. I'm sure to him I was nothing more than a silhouette. A cute silhouette, granted. "But that's the easy part, Sam. If you deliver him to me, I will hurt him. I will do everything within my power to make him feel the pain he has made me feel. But first I will play my wife's last message to him. I want him to hear her voice. I want my wife's voice to be the last thing that son-of-a-bitch hears."

A single prop airplane flew low overhead, its engine droning steadily and peacefully. A bug alighted on my arm. A mosquito. Now there's irony for you. I flicked it off before I inadvertently created a mutant strain of immortal mosquitoes, impervious to bug spray or squishing.

Stuart went on. "But I'm going to give him a fighting chance, more than he gave my wife, the fucking coward. I'm not sure what sort of fighting chance I will give him, but I will think of something."

We were quiet. The woods itself wasn't so quiet. Tree branches swished in the hot wind, and birds twittered and sung and squawked. A quiet hum of life and energy seemed to emanate from everywhere, a gentle combination of every little thing moving and breathing and existing. Sometimes a leaf crunched. Sometimes something fast and little scurried up a trunk. A bird or two flashed overhead, through the tangle of branches. Insects buzzed in and out of the faint, slanting half-light.

Stuart was looking down. A bug had alighted on his bald head, threatening its perfection. He casually reached up and slapped his head, then wiped his palm. Whew! Disaster averted. Stuart, I saw, was crying gently, nearly imperceptively.

I waited by the van. He cried some more, then nodded and wiped his eyes. His whole bald head was gleaming red.

"Let's do this," he said, nodding some more.

"You don't have to do this," I said.

"No, this is the best answer. This is the *only* answer, Sam. I want justice, but the courts won't give it to me."

"Jerry Blum is a professional killer. He's going to know how to fight. And he's going to kill you the first chance he gets."

"I have been taking boxing lessons these past few weeks, since our last talk."

"Boxing lessons where?" I asked.

"A little Irish guy. Says he knows you. Says you're a freak of nature."

"Jacky's always exaggerating," I said.

"Says you knocked out a top-ranked Marine boxer."

"The top-ranked Marine boxer had it coming to him."

Stuart looked at me. The red blotches that had covered his head were dissipating. He looked so gentle and kind and little. I couldn't imagine him taking on a crime lord single-handedly. "You are a fascinating woman, Ms. Moon."

"So they say," I said, and decided to change the subject, especially since the subject was me. "Stuart, there's a very real chance you aren't walking out of this grove alive in a few days."

That seemed to hit him. He thought about it. "Well, this is a good place to die, then, isn't it?"

"You don't have to die, Stuart," I said.

"No," he said. "I suppose I could always just shoot him before he knows what hits him. Or have a whole array of weapons at my disposal."

I said nothing. I was liking this plan less and less.

"But he killed my wife, Sam. He put fear in her. He put terror in her. He made the woman I love feel *terror*. Think about that. He made the woman I loved, the woman I had committed my life to, the woman I was going to start a family with, die in a fiery crash. I hate him. I hate him more than you could ever know. Yes, I suppose I should just step out of the shadows with a gun. I suppose I should just level it at him, and blow his fucking brains out. Maybe I still will. I don't know. But I want to beat him, Sam. With my fists. I want to hear his nose break. I want to see his blood flow. I want to punch him harder than I have ever punched anything in my life. I want to see the terror in *his eyes* when he realizes he will never get up again, that he will die in that moment."

"And when you kill him?" I asked. "What then?"

Stuart turned to me and looked perplexed by the

question. He hadn't, of course, thought much beyond this. A red welt was blistering on the side of his head, where the mosquito had gotten to him a fraction before he had gotten to the mosquito. The blood-sucking little bastard.

"I don't know, Sam. I don't know." He paused, then looked me directly in the eye. "Will you still help me?"

I was never much for vigilante justice. I had taken an oath years ago to uphold the law. This was very much outside the law. This was also crazy.

These are crazy times, I thought.

"Yes," I said. "Of course."

"Thank you, Sam."

And when he said those words, a dull tingling sensation rippled through me, and something very strange happened to the air around Stuart. A very faint, darkish halo briefly surrounded his body. The black halo flared once, twice, and then disappeared.

Chapter Thirty-nine

There was a knock on my hotel door.

Monica, who had been lying on her side and reading, snapped her head around and looked at me.

I stepped away from my laptop and moved over to the bedside table. I quietly pulled open the top drawer and removed my small handgun from its shoulder holster. Then I slipped quietly over and stood to one side of the door. Never directly in front.

"Who's there?" I asked.

"Detective Sherbet."

I grinned. I was quite fond of the detective, who was an aging homicide investigator here in Fullerton. A few months back, Sherbet had helped me solve Kingsley's attempted murder case. And spending long nights sitting together in the rain on stakeouts had gotten us close. But not so close that I had revealed to him my super-secret identity.

I unlocked and opened the door to find the big detective standing there holding a greasy bag of donuts. He was also breathing loudly through his open mouth, and I realized just the effort of walking down the hallway had been a bit much for the old guy. The donuts didn't help.

"Got a minute?" he asked.

"Do I have a choice?" I asked.

"Not really."

"In that case, come in, detective."

He came in, nodded at me, spotted Monica on the bed, and went straight over to her. He took both her hands in his one free hand. The other, of course, was holding the donuts. Monica sat up immediately when she saw him, and now she looked a bit like a teenage girl talking to her grandfather.

"Hello, Monica," he said warmly. "Are you keeping Samantha out of trouble?"

She smiled—or tried to smile—and then she burst into tears. Detective Sherbet calmly set the greasy bag on the night table, then sat next to her and put an arm around her. He made small, comforting noises to her, and they sat like this for a few minutes.

Sherbet squeezed her shoulders one more time, patted her hands, and then stood. He grabbed the bag of donuts and led me out onto the balcony. He closed the sliding glass door behind me. He then sat on one of the dusty, cushioned chairs, calmly opened the oily bag, peered inside, and selected a bright pink donut.

"I thought you didn't like the color pink," I said. "Or, for that matter, pink anything."

"I'm coming around," he said, and held up the effeminate-looking donut.

"Speaking of pink," I said. "How's your son?"

Sherbet paused mid-chew, breathing loudly through his nose. He finished the bite and looked at me sideways. "That was a low blow, Ms. Moon."

"You know I adore your son."

"I do, too," he said. "The kid's fine. I caught him trying on his mother's pantyhose the other day. Pantyhose."

"What did you do?" I asked, suppressing a giggle.

"Honestly? I went into my bedroom, shut the door, and sat in the dark for an hour or two."

"So you took it well."

"About as well as any dad would."

"You love him, though."

Sherbet reached inside the bag again. "In a weird way, I think I love him more."

"Oh?"

He pulled out an apple fritter. Remnants of the pink frosting donut were smeared on the fritter. Sherbet licked the remnants off.

He said, "The kid's going to have it tough in school, and everywhere else, for that matter. He's going to need someone strong by his side."

I patted his roundish knee, hidden beneath slacks that were stretched tight. I think Sherbet had gained 10 or 15 pounds since I'd last seen him. He didn't sound very healthy, either. As he ate the donut, I reached over and gently took the greasy bag from him. He watched in mild shock as I held my hand over the balcony railing.

"Sam, don't," he said.

"You're gaining weight, detective. And you sound like you need a respirator. These things aren't helping."

"You sound like my wife."

"You should listen to her."

I let the bag go. Five seconds later, I heard it splat nine floors below.

Sherbet winced. "I should give you a ticket for littering."

"Then give me a ticket."

He went to work on the rest of the fritter. "My hands are too sticky to write. Besides, I've got some news for you."

"Go ahead."

"We got a call from a guest staying here at the hotel."

Sherbet licked his fingers. I waited.

"She reported that a strange man had been watching the hotel for a few days now. So we sent one of our guys around and talked to him. The guy's story didn't sound kosher, and so we picked him up for questioning."

"And did he answer your questions?"

"Not at first, but, believe it or not, I can play bad cop pretty damn well."

"Bad cop? You? Never!"

Sherbet grinned. There was pink frosting in his cop mustache. I should have told him there was pink frosting in his cop mustache, but he looked so damn cute that I decided not to. "So I shake this guy down and he finally tells me his story."

"He's a hired killer," I said.

"You know the story?"

"I can guess some of it."

"So what else can you guess, Sam?"

"He was hired by Ira Lang."

Sherbet raised his thick finger and shot me. The finger glistened stickily. "Bingo."

Chapter Forty

Detective Sherbet sat back and folded his hairy arms over his roundish stomach.

I mostly wasn't attracted to roundish stomachs and hairy arms—or, for that matter, hairy anything. But on Sherbet, the longish arm hair and extra stomach padding seemed right. On him, oddly, both were attractive. If he had been single and I had been another twenty years older, there was a very good chance I would have had the hots for him.

He seemed to be noticing me looking at his stomach and unconsciously adjusted his shirt over, not realizing that his padded stomach was adding to his manliness. At least for me. I can't vouch for every woman.

I suspected I had daddy issues, whatever that meant.

"He also said something else," said Sherbet. As he spoke, he looked through the sliding glass door at Monica, who was sitting on the edge of the bed and wringing her hands and rocking slightly. I couldn't be sure, but I think she was mumbling something, or singing something. The woman was tormented beyond words, and my heart went out to her.

I looked back at Sherbet, "What else?"

"He told me that Ira Lang would never give up trying to kill her, that Lang had approached many, many people in prison, and that just because we caught him once, didn't mean we were going to catch the next killer that Ira hired, or the next, or the next."

"He's going to keep coming after her," I said. "Forever, until one or the other dies."

"Which, for him, is sooner rather than later, since he's on Death Row."

"Still a few years away, though."

"Or longer," said Sherbet. "Unless, of course, you visit him again, in which case he might not survive the meeting."

"He threatened the kids."

"You are a mama grizzly."

"I'm a mama something."

Sherbet looked at me, seemed about to say something, paused, then seemed to go a different direction. "Anyway, he's out of the hospital and back on Death Row."

"Where he belongs."

"I couldn't agree more."

We were silent. Sherbet's overtaxed digestive

system moaned pitifully as it went to work on the greasy donuts.

"Which reminds me," said Sherbet, reaching down and opening his briefcase. He extracted a smallish electronic gizmo thingy. "I want to show you something."

"Your new DVD player?" I asked.

He grinned. "Sort of. It's a loaner from the department."

I watched with mild amusement as his sausage-like fingers tried to manipulate the small piece of electronic gadgetry. He picked it up and examined it from every angle.

"Everything's so damned small," he grumbled.

"Let me have a look, detective," I said. He gratefully handed it to me. I took it from him, and flipped a switch on the side and the player whirred to life.

"Should I press 'play'?" I asked.

"Yes," he said.

I set the player on the table between us and pressed 'play', and a moment later I saw a sickening scene. It was footage from a security camera, looking down on two people conversing in a jail visiting room. Both were on the phone, speaking to each other through a thick, bulletproof glass window.

Sherbet was watching me closely as the video played on the little screen. I hate being watched closely. My first instinct was to turn the damn thing off and fling it over the balcony railing like I had with the donuts.

My next instinct was to make a joke or two about the video, perhaps something about the camera adding ten pounds. But there was no joking my way out of this.

I had been wrong: there *was* a camera in the jail's visiting room, perhaps hidden.

Besides, I felt too sick to joke, so instead I watched the tape with horror and curiosity. After all, it was a rare day that I actually got to see myself.

Of course, I had worn a lot of make-up that night, knowing there would security cameras everywhere, and wanting to make sure I didn't show up as partially invisible. In fact, anytime I was anywhere that had heightened video security, I made it a point to wear extra make-up.

Anyway, the video was grainy at best. No sound, either. On the tiny screen, I watched as I sat forward in the chair, speaking deliberately to Ira. Ira was leaning some of his weight on his elbows and didn't seem to blink. Ever. I hadn't noticed that before. Then again, that could have been a result of this grainy image. The camera had been filming from above, in the upper corner of the visitor's side of the room.

From this angle, I could see some of my profile, and I watched myself, fascinated, despite my mounting dread over what was about to come.

In the video, I looked leaner than I had ever looked in my life. A good thing, I guess. I also looked strong, vibrant. I didn't look like the stereotypical sickly vampire. But I knew that wasn't always the case. This was early evening. I always looked better in the early evening. Or so I was told.

And, if I do say so myself, I looked striking. Not beautiful. But striking.

As the video played out, I must have said something with some finality because I ducked my head slightly and reached for my purse. As I did so, Ira said something to me, and I immediately sat back down again. I leaned closer to the window. Ira did, too, grinning stupidly from behind the protective glass.

Now my face looked terrible. I suddenly didn't look like me. Truth be known, I didn't recognize the woman in the video clip at all. She seemed strange, otherworldly. Her mannerisms seemed a little off, too. She moved very little, if at all. Every movement controlled, planned, or rehearsed. In fact, the woman in the video seemed content sitting perfectly still.

But now I wasn't sitting still. Now I was motioning with my finger for Ira to come ever closer. And he did.

One moment I was sitting there, and the next I was reaching through the destroyed glass, grabbing Ira, slamming his face over and over into the glass. What I saw didn't make sense, either. A smallish woman reaching through the glass, manhandling a grown man, a convict, a killer. Slamming him repeatedly against the glass as if he were a rag doll.

None of it made sense; it defied explanation.

It defied *normal* explanation.

A moment later the guards burst into the room. The final clip was an image I had not seen since I was struggling under a sea of guards. It was an image of Ira's face, partially pulled through the glass, his skin having been peeled away from his forehead like a sardine can. Also, the glass was cutting deeply into his throat, and he was jerking violently, gagging on his own blood, which flowed freely down the glass, spilling over both sides of the counter, dripping, dripping. He would have surely died within minutes if he had not been given emergency help.

Sherbet reached over and easily turned off the player and sat back, watching me some more. He said, "The guards reported that you were nearly impossible to tackle to the ground. That it took three of them to do so, and even then you wouldn't go down easily."

I said nothing. For some reason, I was remembering what I had looked like in the security video. My passive expression. My inert features.

Sherbet went on, "As you can see in the video, you punched through the glass so fast that there was little or no indication that you moved at all. One moment you're sitting there, and the next you are reaching through the glass. We were certain the digital video had skipped a few seconds ahead, but the timer on it never missed a beat. One second you are sitting there. Two-tenths of a second later you are reaching through the glass. Two-tenths of a second, faster than a blink of an eye. And during those two-tenths, you are seen flinching only slightly. The broken glass itself can be seen hurling through the air at the same time you are holding Ira by the neck." Sherbet shook his head. "It defies all explanation. It defies natural law."

Beyond my hotel balcony, the sky was alive with streaking particles of light, flashing faintly in every direction. Thank God I can mostly ignore these flashing lights, or I would go crazy. Vampirism and OCD do not mix.

Sherbet looked at me. "Do you have anything to say about this, Samantha?"

I continued looking up at the night sky, at the dancing lights. No jokes, no nothing. I needed this to go away. "Obviously there was something wrong with the video, Detective."

He nodded his head as if he had expected that answer. "And the fact that you broke through the security glass?"

"The glass was already broken."

"We can't see any breaks in the image."

"You yourself said the image is not the clearest."

He nodded again. Now he turned his head and looked in the same direction I was looking. I doubted he could see the zigzagging lights.

I asked, "Why were you shown the video?"

Sherbet chuckled lightly. "Are you kidding, Sam? The video has made its way through our entire department. Hell, half the police in the state have seen it by now. You're lucky it's not on BoobTube."

"YouTube," I said, and thought I was going to vomit. So much for keeping things on the down-low.

Sherbet went on, "You can imagine my surprise when I discovered the freak in the video was, in fact, you."

"Probably so surprised that you nearly dropped your donut," I said.

"I'm never that surprised."

"So why are you here?" I asked.

"Just chatting with an old friend."

"I'm not so old," I said.

He nodded as if that somehow answered a question he had. Now we were both silent. Inside the hotel, Monica had turned on the TV—a comedy show judging by the sudden bursts of laughter. Monica giggled innocently.

"I'm your friend, Sam."

"I know."

"Anything you tell me will remain between us."

"Anything?"

"Anything."

"That's good to know," I said.

"I worry about you, Sam."

The surprising tenderness in his gravelly voice touched me deeply, and I found words temporarily impossible to form. I nodded. My vision blurred into tears.

"If you ever want to talk," he said. "If you ever need a friend. If you ever need help of any kind, I'm always here for you. Always."

And now I was weeping.

He reached over and hugged me tight, pulling me into him, and I smelled his after shave and the donut grease and the smallest hint of body odor. The body odor went with the manliness. After all, this was the end of a long day of crime fighting. A man *should* have a hint of body odor at the end of a long day.

His hairy arms smothered me completely and for a few seconds, a few rare seconds, I felt safe and comfortable and cared for.

Then he pulled away and carefully packed up his mini-DVD player in his scuffed briefcase. He then gave me the softest jab you could ever imagine on my chin, smiled sadly at me, and left me on the balcony.

Inside the hotel room, through the sliding glass door, I watched as he quietly spoke to Monica. As he did so, he held both of her hands in one of his. He said something else, jerked his head in my direction, and she nodded. He was reassuring her, I knew. Letting her know she was in good hands.

When the door shut behind him, Monica came out and sat beside me. She reached over and took my hand, and we sat like that for a few minutes.

Finally, I said, "They caught a guy hanging around downstairs."

"The guy Ira hired to hurt me." Her voice

sounded so tiny and lost and confused. Her simple, sweet, innocent brain was trying to wrap itself around why a man she had loved at one time would actually hire another man to hurt her. To kill her.

And as we sat out there together, as we held hands and watched the quarter moon climb slowly into the hazy night sky, I suddenly knew what I had to do.

Chapter Forty-one

I was flying. I was free. Life was good.

The moon, still about a week from being full, shone high and bright. Any thoughts of the moon automatically conjured images of Kingsley. And any thoughts of Kingsley automatically conjured images of the beast he was, or claimed to be. Admittedly, I had never actually seen Kingsley transform into a werewolf, and a part of me still wanted to believe that, in fact, he *wasn't* a werewolf, that this was all one crazy hoax. Or that he was delusional.

I mean, come on, an honest-to-God werewolf? Really?

This, of course, coming from a creature flying slowly over Orange County.

Actually, a part of me—a big part—still hoped that I was in the middle of one long, horrific nightmare, and that I would wake up at any moment, in bed, gasping, relieved beyond words that this had all been one bad dream.

I'm ready to wake up, I thought. *Please.*

I banked to port and caught a high-altitude wind. I flapped my wings easily, smoothly, comfortably, sailing along in the heavens like an escaped Macy's Thanksgiving Day Parade float from Hell.

Still, just because one monster (me) existed, that didn't necessarily mean all *other* monsters existed.

Or did it? Maybe there was some truth to everything that goes bump-in-the-night. If so, where did it end? Were there fairies? Angels? Aliens? Demons? Keebler elves? And weren't elves, in fact, fairies? Or was it the other way around?

I didn't know.

More than likely Kingsley was exactly what he claimed to be: a werewolf. I had seen the excessive hair on his forearms a few times now. I had also seen him survive five bullet shots to the head. Not to mention, he didn't even bat an eye when he found out that I was, in fact, a vampire.

Still, that didn't a werewolf make.

The moon burned silver above me. I wondered if I could fly all the way to the moon. I wondered if I could fly to other worlds, too.

Maybe someday I will fly to the moon.

Dance on the Moon.

I hadn't spoken to Kingsley in a few nights now, not since I had discovered that he was, in fact, responsible for getting Ira out of jail. Jesus, how do you respect a man who does that for a living?

An icy wind blasted me, but I held my course. I flapped steadily, powerfully into the night.

Granted, not all of Kingsley's clients were killers. Some were innocent. Some he legitimately helped. Others, not so much. Others were evil and wretched and should stay in jail. Kingsley knew damn well that he was releasing animals back into society, that he was putting killers back onto the streets.

But I had known this about Kingsley already, hadn't I? It hadn't really bothered me until now. *Until it hit close to home.* So why should I hold it against him now? Kingsley had done nothing wrong. Hell, he was just doing his job. Like he said, if it hadn't been him, it would have been another defense attorney getting Ira out of jail.

So perhaps I should be angry at the system, not Kingsley.

Perhaps.

Below me was my destination. It was a massive multi-storied structure in Chino, California. It lay sprawled before me in a hodgepodge of auxiliary wings and isolated buildings. My target was one of those isolated buildings, located on the north side of the prison.

The Death Row Compound.

It was a large, grim, three-story structure that housed hundreds of condemned inmates. A lethal, electrified fence encircled the compound. Guard towers were everywhere.

I circled the bleak structure once, twice, getting a feel for the place. I circled again a third time, and as I did so, I felt a pull for a particular area. I focused on that area as I circled the structure again.

The pull grew stronger.

I rarely used my new-found psychic ability in this way. In the past, I just sifted through various hits as they came, rarely directing my heightened senses.

Now I directed them.

I was searching for one inmate in particular. One inmate currently housed in Death Row. One inmate who's time had come.

As I circled the structure a fifth time, I felt a very strong pull toward a corner wall on the second floor.

There he is, I thought.

I knew it. I felt it. I believed it.

But what if I was wrong?

I let the question die in me unanswered; I didn't have the luxury of being wrong.

As I circled back from my fifth fly-by, I tucked in my leathery wings and dove down, fast, the wind howling over my flattened ears.

Chapter Forty-two

As I rapidly approached the building, I was suddenly filled with doubt. Was I doing the right thing? Should I veer off now and forget this whole crazy, horrific, stomach-turning plan? Was I even heading toward the right section of prison?

I shook my head and blasted aside the self-doubt.

The decisions had been made hours ago, and I knew, in my heart, they were the right ones.

Now, of course, it only remained to be seen if I was heading towards the correct section of prison wall.

We'll see, I thought.

I flew faster. The west side of the wall grew rapidly before me. I adjusted my wings slightly, a flick here, a dip there, and angled toward a particular spot on the second floor, near the corner of the building.

It just feels right.

I picked up more speed. The massive, oppressive structure grew rapidly in front of me. Behind those walls were the worst of the worst. Killers, cutthroats, and the not very kind. Wind thundered over me, screeching across my ears.

There was a final moment when I could have chosen to veer away, and avoid the building altogether.

I didn't veer away.

Six years ago, I was busting loan swindlers and thieves and low lives. Now I was hurling my nightmarish bat-like body at a maximum security prison.

Would this kill me? I didn't know, but I was about to find out.

My last thought before I struck the wall were: *I love you Tammy and Anthony...if I don't make it, I'll see you on the other side.*

The gray wall appeared directly before me. I could see the fine details of thick cinder blocks and heavy bricks. I lowered my head and turned my body slightly and struck the building with such force that I suspected the whole damn building shuddered.

***

I sat up in a pile of rubble.

My thick wings were draped around me like a heavy, dusty blanket. Chunks of wall continued to fall and clatter behind me. I should have been dead many times over. I should have been flattened outside on the wall itself. I should have been many things...but here I sat, in a prison cell, surrounded by massive chunks of cement, bent re-bar, and bricks that looked better suited for a medieval dungeon.

As I sat up, and as the dust still settled around me, I closed my eyes and saw the single flame in my forethoughts. I next saw the woman in the flame, standing there impatiently, and quickly I felt the familiar *rush* towards her....

And when I opened my eyes, there I was. My old self again—completely naked in a maximum secure prison in a cell on Death Row.

Outside, through the massive hole in the prison wall, I heard dozens of men shouting and a cacophony of running feet. A moment later, a siren wailed, so loud that it hurt even my ears.

I stood slowly. Dust and debris slid off my flesh.

Had I guessed right? Was this the right cell? Had my sixth sense led me to the man I wanted?

My eyes needed no time to adjust to the darkness.

There, huddled at the far end of the single cot, was Ira Lang, staring at me with wild, disbelieving eyes. *Believe it, buddy boy.* Ira was a royal mess. His face and forehead were nearly covered in bandages, and if it weren't for his signature bald head, with its deep grooves and odd lumps, I might have wondered if I had the right room. His face, what little of it I could see puffing out between the bandages, was horribly swollen and disfigured. A multitude of pins and bolts and screws were holding the whole thing together.

What a waste, I thought, *of all that work.*

There was no way of knowing what Ira was thinking. Hell, what could he be thinking? One moment he was lying in bed, no doubt plotting his ex-wife's death, or perhaps sleeping, and dreaming of her death, and the next a massive hole appears in his jail cell, filled by a hulking, nightmarish creature. A creature who then turned into a woman. A woman he loathed.

I didn't know what he thought, nor did I care.

I brushed off some dirt and smaller chunks of concrete from my shoulder and shook out cement dust from my hair. A small, grayish cloud briefly hovered around me, and then drifted to the floor.

People were shouting within the prison itself, their voices echoing along what I assumed was a long hallway just beyond. Lights were still out. No one could see me. No one, but Ira.

Now he was blinking at me hard. He then sat forward a little, straining to see through the dark and dust. He breathed raspily through his misshapen and swollen mouth.

Footsteps pounded from somewhere nearby. Sirens blasted from seemingly everywhere. A spotlight flashed through the opening, catching some of the swirling dust.

Ira's eyes widened some more. "You!" he suddenly hissed. His swollen lips never moved, and the sound itself seemed to come from somewhere in his throat. "How the fuck did you get in here?"

I said nothing. There was nothing to say. Things were about to end badly for Ira and there was no reason to joke or elaborate or waste time.

I stood there, waiting, naked as the day I was born. I was certain most of my body was silhouetted by the lights coming in through the large opening in the wall behind me. How much Ira could see of me, I didn't know, nor did I care.

I don't think he cared either.

He reached underneath his flimsy bed mattress, and then hurled himself at me. As he did so, I spotted something flashing in his hands. Growling with what could have been demonic rage, he drove the metal object—which turned out to be a sharpened spoon wired to a wooden stick—as hard as he could at my chest. Whether or not the shank qualified as a stake, I didn't know, nor did I want to find out. I caught his slashing wrist as he slammed into me hard. I stumbled back a foot or two and nearly tripped on a block of cement, but mostly I held my ground. Ira brought his knee up hard into my stomach. Air burst from my lungs. He redoubled his effort with the shank, and I might have squeezed his wrist a little too hard, because I felt bones crunching. As Ira screamed, I spun him around and reached up with one hand and grabbed his already broken jaw and turned his head as hard and fast as I could. I nearly ripped his head off. His neck broke instantly, sickeningly, the vertebrae tearing through his skin and his orange prison jumpsuit like jagged shards of broken glass. Ira shuddered violently, and then went limp. His head fell grotesquely to one side.

More sirens. More running feet. Now lights were turning on in the prison itself.

They were coming for me. At any moment, someone was going to burst into this cell. I had to leave now. But I didn't. Not yet. Instead, I found myself staring down at Ira's broken neck. I wanted to drink from him so bad that I was willing to risk getting caught. I was willing to give it all up for one drink of fresh blood.

More footsteps. Just outside of the door.

I tore my gaze away, gasping, and dropped Ira's lifeless body to the debris-strewn floor. I moved quickly over to the hole in the wall, took a deep breath, and jumped.

Chapter Forty-three

Separating Chino and Orange is Chino State Park, which really isn't much of a park. Mostly it's a long stretch of barren hills. The hills are full of coyotes, rabbits, and the occasional mountain lion. And tonight, at least, one giant vampire bat.

I alighted on the roundish summit of the highest hill. From here I could see the lights of North Orange County twinkling beautifully. I folded my wings in and hunkered down on the lip of a rocky overhang.

The wind was strong up here, buffeting me steadily, slapping my wings gently against my side. Something small scurried in the grass nearby. That something popped its little head up and looked at me. A squirrel. It studied me for a moment, cocking its head, and then scurried off in a blink.

Well, excuse me.

The cool night wind carried with it the heady scent of juniper and sage, and I sat silently on that ledge and stared down into Orange County and remembered the feeling of the man's neck breaking in my hands.

Grass rustled in the wind. My wings continued flapping. Grains of sand sprinkled against my thick hide. A hazy gauze of clouds crawled in front of the moon, nudged along by the high winds.

In my mind's eye, I summoned the leaping flame, summoned the woman within. I opened my eyes a few seconds later and found myself squatting over the ledge, my long dark hair whipping in the wind, my elbows tucked against my sides.

I buried my face in my hands and wanted to cry, but I couldn't cry. I couldn't cry because something had changed within me tonight, something so damn frightening I could barely acknowledge it.

But I had to acknowledge it.

Tonight, as I had held Ira's broken body close to me, I had loved every minute of it. Every fucking second of it. It had been such a thrill killing him.

Fuck.

Double fuck.

The scariest part of tonight was that his killing had felt incomplete. Foreplay, without the pay-off. I had wanted to drink from that broken neck. Desperately. Passionately. Endlessly. Draining every drop of blood.

Sweet Jesus, help me.

I reached down and picked up a handful of cool

desert sand. I let the fine granules sift through my fingers and catch on the wind, to be carried off to distant lands and far shores, even if those distant lands were just Orange County and those far shores were heated pools.

I reached up with both hands and covered my head and closed my eyes and listened to the wind and the critters and the swishing grass, and stayed liked that for a long, long time...

Chapter Forty-four

I killed a man tonight.

There was a long pause, then Fang wrote: *Are you sure you want to tell me about this here?*

Big Brother?

Big something. You've stirred things up enough that someone, somewhere, might be watching and listening.

I doubt it, I wrote.

Your sixth sense?

Something like that.

You don't feel like anyone's watching?

No, I wrote. *Not yet. Maybe someday I will have to be more careful.*

But not now?

No.

Can we be careful for my benefit? he wrote.

Sure. We can pretend I killed a man tonight.

That's better. Pretend is better. Why did you

pretend to kill him?

Because he was a bad man.

You can't kill all the bad men, Moon Dance. What did he do that was so bad?

I told Fang about it, writing up the case quickly, hitting just the high notes. Two seconds after I hit "Send", Fang was already writing me back.

Someone had to die, Moon Dance. Better him than your client.

We were both silent for a long, long time. I tried to imagine what Fang was doing at this moment. Probably sitting back and studying my words. Probably drinking from a bottle of beer, although he had never mentioned if he drank beer or not. *Call it a hunch.* I imagined Fang taking a long pull on his beer, maybe crossing one leg over the other, maybe reaching down and scratching his crotch, as guys are wont to do.

He wrote, *Does your client know about the killing?*

Not yet.

Where is she now?

With me in bed, sleeping.

You sleep together?

Get your mind out of the gutter. This is the first time she has slept so deeply since I have been protecting her.

People are more psychic than they realize. Perhaps a part of her knows she is finally safe.

But I had to kill a man to keep her safe.

Better him than her.

Tonight I had bought a pack of cigarettes. I opened the package and tapped one out and lit it with a lighter. The tip flared and the acrid smell of burning paper and tobacco reached my nose nearly instantly. I loved the initial scent of a freshly lit cigarette, even if I wasn't smoking it. I looked down at the burning cancer stick. It was my first cigarette since before I was pregnant. I had given up smokes completely, being a good preggo. I had thought I had given them up for good, but with the fear of cancer removed, well, what the hell? Why not? I just wouldn't smoke them around my kids. Or if I was about to kiss a man.

I've never killed before, I wrote.

How do you feel?

I sucked on the cigarette and thought about that. *I feel nothing.*

No guilt?

No. Not right now, but it might hit me later.

How did you feel when you were killing him?

Why do you ask?

It is commonly believed that vampires enjoy the kill, that vampires sort of get-off on taking another's life.

I took another hit, inhaling deeply, and came clean. *I enjoyed it so fucking much that it scares the shit out of me.*

Because you might want to do it again?

Exactly.

Did you feed from him?

No. I didn't have time. But I think I would have.

I paused, then added: *And now tonight feels incomplete.*

Because you didn't feed?

Right.

You hunted your prey...and then lost him to the hyenas.

I shuddered at the imagery. *Something like that.*

Can you control yourself, Moon Dance?

I nodded, even though he couldn't see me nod. *Yes, the feeling passed as soon as I left the cell.*

A good thing it passed.

I nodded again. I knew what Fang meant. If the hunger hadn't passed, if it still gripped me, there was a very good chance that something else—or someone else—would be very dead tonight.

Do you think of me differently, Fang?

Do you think of yourself differently?

I finished the cigarette, stubbed it out in the glass ashtray on the night stand next to me. *I've never killed before. Anyone or anything. I always had that to fall back on. Now I don't.*

Now you're a killer.

Yes.

You killed a bad man who, if given a chance, would have hurt or killed your client.

Yes.

So, in effect, you acted in self-defense of your client.

You could say that.

You had asked him politely to leave her alone, and what did he do?

He threatened me and my children.

So, in effect, you also protected your children.

I'm not sure how serious his threats were.

The man was on Death Row, Moon Dance.

But I still killed him in cold blood, Fang.

That is something you will have to live with, Moon Dance. Can you live with it?

I guess I have to.

An eternity is a long time to carry guilt, Moon Dance.

Our fingers were both silent. I contemplated another cigarette, then decided against it. Now Fang was busy writing something, and so I waited for his response. A minute later, it came.

You did what you had to do. You acted in the best interest of yourself, your kids and your client. You rid the world of an animal who made it his life's goal to destroy other people's lives. You ask me, you had a pretty good night's work.

We were silent for a long time. I gazed out the sliding glass window at the rising moon. I turned back to my laptop.

Get some sleep, Fang.

You know I'm a night owl, Moon Dance.

Yeah, I know.

See you in a week?

My heart pounded once, twice in my chest.

Yes, in a week.

I can't wait, Moon Dance.

I bit my lip. *Neither can I.*

Chapter Forty-five

I was boxing with Jacky.

It was late afternoon and I was tired and my hands kept dropping. Jacky hated when my hands dropped and he let me know it. I was working on a punching bag while he stood behind it, absorbing my blows. Each punch seemed to knock the little Irishman off balance a little more. I had learned not to hit the bag with all my strength, or even half my strength, as such blows would send the little man rebounding off the bag as if it had been an electrified fence.

Even in the late afternoon, with the sun not fully set and my strength nowhere near where it could be, my punches had a lot of pop behind them.

I'm such a freak.

And as Jacky worked me in three minute drills —equivalent to boxing rounds—I was pouring sweat. I sometimes wondered what my sweat would look like under a microscope. Was it the same as anyone else's sweat? Was my DNA vastly different? Would a lab technician, studying my little squigglies under the lens, shit his pants if he saw what I was really made up of?

And what was I made up of? *Who knows.*

Still, it gave me an idea. A very interesting idea. Hmm...

"Hands up, wee girl. Hands—"

I hit the bag hard, so hard that it rebounded back into Jacky's face and caused him, I think, to bite his lip. Oops. He cursed and held on tight, but at least he shut the hell up about my damn hands.

Easy girl. He's just doing his job.

I was in a mood. A foul mood. I needed to punch something and punch it hard, but I didn't want to hurt Jacky. A conundrum, for sure.

And as I wrapped up the fourteenth round, finishing in a flurry of punches that made Jacky, no doubt, regret taking me on as a client, Detective Sherbet stepped into the gym. The heavy-set detective looked around, blinking hard, eyes adjusting to the gloom, spotted me, and then motioned for me to come over. I told Jacky I would be back, and the little Irishman, wiping the blood from his lip, seemed only too relieved to be rid of me for a few minutes.

I grabbed a towel and soon the detective and I were sitting on a bench in the far corner of the gym. I was sweating profusely and continuously drying myself. Sherbet was wearing slacks and a nice shirt.

There was a fresh jelly stain near one of the buttons. The buttons were doing all they could to contain his girth.

"You sweat a lot for a girl," he said.

"I've heard that before."

Sherbet grinned. "It's not necessarily a bad thing."

"I've heard that before, too. So how did you find me, Detective?"

"I happen to be an ace investigator. That, and Monica told me."

I nodded. "And to what do I owe the honor?"

Sherbet was looking at me closely, and perhaps a little oddly. If I had to put a name to it, I would say he was looking at me *suspiciously*.

He said, "Ira Lang is dead."

"What a shame."

"You don't seem surprised."

"I'm too tired to seem surprised," I said. "There's a reason for all this sweat, you know."

"Don't you care how he died?"

"No."

"His neck was broken."

I made a noncommittal sound. Sherbet interlaced his fingers and formed a sort of human cup with the palms of his hands. He tapped the tips of his thumbs together. Nearby, somebody was kicking a heavy bag with a lot of power.

"It happened last night, in his cell."

I kept saying nothing. Sweat continued to drip, and I continued to mop my brow. I didn't look at

Sherbet.

The detective said, "There was an explosion of some type, which blasted a hole into his cell. Crazy, I know, but someone broke into his cell."

"You're not making sense, Detective."

"None of it makes sense, Sam. Whatever broke into his cell appears to have killed him, as well. Nearly ripped his head clean off."

I listened to a woman *hi-yah-ing!* with her trainer, grunting the word with each kick or punch. I wanted to *hi-yah* her face.

"Prison officials don't know what to make of it. The explosion rocked the whole building. Everyone felt it, even those a few buildings away felt it. But there was no evidence of an explosion. It was as if a massive cannonball had been launched at the wall."

"Detective, if I didn't know better, I would say you've been sneaking in some of the hard stuff during your lunch breaks."

He mostly ignored me, although he might have cracked a smile. "They're keeping it out of the press. They have to. Something like this can't get out. Besides, what do they report?"

"So Ira is really dead?"

"Yes."

"And this story of yours is real?"

"So far, it's not much of a story. The warden and his men have no clue what happened."

"And there were no witnesses?"

"Oh, there was a witness."

"What did he see?"

"A guard working the tower heard the explosion. Everyone did. He started looking for the source and found the gaping hole in the Death Row wing. A moment later, he sees what he claims is a naked woman jump from the opening." I burst out laughing, but Sherbet ignored me and continued on. "The guard had been in the process of reporting the hole to the warden when the woman jumped out of Ira's cell. The guard was a fraction of a second too late getting back to his light. The woman disappeared and the last he reports is something quite large and black flew directly over the tower. The woman was never found."

"Was she seen on video?"

"The video they have shows the wall caving in from an unknown impact. An invisible impact. Nothing else can be seen. Nothing inside, since the angle was wrong. And not the woman or whatever the guard had seen flying overhead."

"Did he say what the woman looked like?" I asked.

"He did. Slender. Long black hair. Pale skin. Did a swan dive out of the hole in the wall."

"Any DNA evidence left behind at the scene?"

"None so far, but they're working on it."

I nodded. "And how do you know all of this?"

"Warden is a friend of mine. Ira was my business. And I'm an acquaintance of yours, a woman who had physically assaulted Ira just a week and a half earlier."

"I'm just an acquaintance? I'm hurt."

Sherbet had been watching me closely during this whole exchange. I had been watching two women sparring in the center ring. Both women looked like they would have trouble punching through a wet paper towel. One of them actually turned and ran, squealing.

"There was something else on the video."

Uh, oh. "Please tell me you didn't bring another portable DVD player," I said.

Sherbet chuckled. "No. I learned my lesson with that damned thing. I'll summarize for you. Just after the explosion, the video captured something else. Granted, the camera was only partially facing the wall—and at this time, the spotlight wasn't yet on the hole in the wall—but we can see what appears to be broken bricks and rocks rising in the air and falling on their own."

"Maybe the prison is haunted," I said.

"If I had to guess, I would say it looked like someone—or something—was getting up from the floor. And the chunks of wall were falling away from the body."

"An *invisible* body," I reminded.

That stopped him. He ducked his head and rubbed his face and groaned a little. He turned and looked at me a moment later, and the poor guy looked truly tortured. The confident detective was gone, replaced by a man who was truly searching for answers.

"What do you make of all that, Sam?" he asked.

"I think someone invisible might have killed

Ira," I said.

"Maybe. Is there anything else you would like to add?"

"It's a wild story, Detective," I said, standing. "You boys might want to keep it to yourselves. You wouldn't want the rest of the world thinking that invisible assassins are killing prisoners at Chino State Prison."

I hated lying to the detective, but I had been lying for so long now about my condition it truly came as second nature for me. Still, I hated to see the confused anguish on his face.

Sherbet nodded and looked at his empty hands. I think he was wishing a big fat donut was in one of those hands. Or both hands. The detective nodded some more, this time to himself, I think, and then stood. As he stood, his knees popped so loudly that a girl walking by snapped her head around and looked at us.

The detective looked down at me and said, "I still have questions for you, Sam."

"And I'm still here, Detective."

He nodded and left, limping slightly.

Chapter Forty-six

Monica and I were in my hotel room, sitting crossed-legged in the center of the bed, holding hands. I had just told her that her husband of thirteen years, a husband who had twice tried to kill her and who, in fact, succeeded in killing her father, was dead. I left out the facts of his death. I told her only that her ex-husband had died suddenly.

Very suddenly, I thought.

Amazingly, Monica broke down. She cried hard for a long, long time. Sometimes I wondered if she even knew *why* she was crying. I suspected that emotions—many different emotions—were sweeping through her, purging her, one set of emotions blending into another, causing more and more tears, until at last she had cried herself out, and now we sat holding hands in the center of the bed.

"So there's no one trying to hurt me anymore?" she finally asked.

"No one's trying to hurt you," I promised. In fact, Detective Sherbet had just sent me a very choppy and error-filled text message (I could just see his thick sausage fingers hunting and pecking over his cell's tiny keyboard) that he had had a heart-to-heart with the accused hitman. The hitman, currently awaiting arraignment for conspiracy to attempt murder, understood that his employer—in this case Ira Lang—was dead.

The hotel was oddly quiet, even to my ears. No elevator sounds. No creaking. No laughing. And no squeaking bed springs.

After a moment, Monica said, "I can't believe he's dead."

I remembered the way Ira's head had dropped to the side, held in place by only the skin of his neck. I had no problem believing he was dead.

"So I guess you're done protecting me?" she added.

"Yes," I said. "But I'm not done being your friend. If you ever need anything, call me. If you're ever afraid, call me. If you ever need help in any way, call me. If you ever want to go dancing, call me."

She laughed, but mostly she cried some more and now she leaned into me and hugged me, and when she pulled away, she looked at me closely.

"Your hands are always cold," she said, her tiny voice barely above a whisper.

"Yes. I'm always cold."

"Always?"

I thought about that. Yeah, I was usually cold, except when I was flush with blood, especially fresh blood. I kept that part to myself.

"Is that part of your sickness?" she asked.

"Yes."

"I'm so sorry you're sick, Samantha."

"So am I."

She held my hands even tighter in a show of solidarity. And like a small child who's always looking to make things better, she swung my hands out a little. "Did you really mean the part about dancing?"

"Sure," I said. "I haven't been dancing in a long time."

"I'm a good dancer," she said.

"I bet you are."

There was a knock on the door, and I got up and checked the peephole and let Chad in. He came bearing flowers and wearing nice cologne. I mentioned something about the flowers being for me and he said in my dreams. My ex-partner was in love, but certainly not with me. I looked over at Monica who brightened immediately at the sight of Chad, or perhaps the flowers. Whether or not she was in love, I didn't know, but, I think, she was in a better place to explore such feelings. In the least, she was now free to love.

Chad pulled me aside and we briefly discussed Ira's crazy death. He wanted to know if I had any additional information and I told him I didn't. We both agreed Ira's death was crazy as hell and both wondered what had happened. We concluded that we may never know, and it was doubtful the prison was coming clean with all the facts. We both concluded that there was some sort of cover-up going on. The cover-up idea was mine, admittedly.

Chad looked at me, but I could tell he was itching to get back to Monica, who was currently inhaling every flower in the bouquet. Chad said, "She'll be safe with me. Always."

"That's good."

"I won't let anyone ever hurt her."

"You are a good man."

"I love her."

"I'm glad to hear it."

"Do you think she loves me?"

"I don't know," I said. "But I think the two of you are off to a great start."

He nodded enthusiastically. "Yeah, I do too."

The two of them left, together, arm-in-arm, and I suddenly found myself alone in my hotel room for the first time in a few weeks. I went out to my balcony and lit a cigarette and stared silently up at the pale, nearly full moon.

My thoughts were all over the place. I was hungry. Starving, in fact. I hadn't eaten in days. I thought of the chilled packets of blood in my hotel refrigerator and made a face, nearly gagging at the thought.

My scattered thoughts eventually settled on

Stuart, my bald client. And I kept thinking about him even as my forgotten cigarette finally burned itself out.

Chapter Forty-seven

I was taking a hot shower.

No doubt it was too hot for most people, but it was just right for me. In fact, if I didn't know better, I would say that I could almost smell my own cooking flesh. Anyway, such hot showers were some of the few times that I could actually feel real heat radiating from my body. The heat would last all of twenty minutes after stepping out of the shower, granted, but beggars couldn't be choosers.

I did my best thinking in the shower, and I was thinking my ass off now. Danny had two things on me: First, he had a vial of blood he had supposedly drawn while I was sleeping (the piece of shit), and, second, he had pictures of me *not* showing up in a mirror, or on the film itself.

Allegedly.

Both items were currently with an attorney friend of his—*allegedly*—who kept them God-knows-where. How much his attorney friend knew about me and my condition, I didn't know, but I doubted Danny told him very much, if anything. Danny was good at keeping secrets. Anyway, according to my ex-husband, his attorney friend had been given strict instructions to make public the files should Danny meet an unfortunate end.

Briefly distracted by picturing Danny's unfortunate end, I allowed the image to play out for exactly six seconds before I forced myself back to reality. However much I hated my ex, he was still the father of my children.

For that, he has been given asylum.

For now.

Anyway, Danny had also threatened to go public with his evidence should I fight him on anything. And so I didn't fight him on anything. And so I accepted his harsh terms, his mental anguish.

I took it, and I took it, and took it.

I was sick of taking it.

So what could I do about it? I thought about that, turning my body in the shower, letting the spray hit me between my shoulder blades. Danny's evidence was centered around my blood. Danny assumed, wrongly or not, that my blood would be different, and that I could be proven to be a monster. He also had the pictures. I wasn't worried about those. Hell, anyone could manipulate such pictures nowadays, and I doubted anyone would take them seriously. Danny would look like a complete idiot waving those pictures around and would be laughed out of a job.

So I could dismiss the pictures.

But could I dismiss the blood? I didn't think so. At least, not yet. The blood worried me. I needed more information. And as the superheated spray worked its way over me, I thought about what I had to do.

A few minutes later, dried and dressed, I grabbed my car keys and headed for the elevator.

It was time for a Wal-Mart run.

***

Two hours later, I was back in my bathroom, this time pouring the contents of a plastic bottle of organic juice down the toilet. Wasteful, I know, but what the hell was I going to do with it? Anyway, I flushed the whole shebang down the pooper, as Anthony would call it, and spent the next few minutes thoroughly cleaning out the container in the bathroom sink. I used my hair dryer to carefully dry the plastic without melting it.

Once done, I carefully cleaned my right index fingernail, running hot water over it and using some hand soap. I next swabbed some rubbing alcohol on my forearm, blew the spot dry, and then carefully pressed my right fingernail into the skin of my arm. I didn't bother to look for a vein. A phlebotomist would have been horrified. Which, by the way, would be a good job for a vampire.

Except you would probably be fired for drinking on the job.

I laughed nervously at my own lame joke while I continued to work my nail deeper into my flesh. A knife would have been good, except I didn't have one handy. Besides, my nail worked just fine.

The first thick drop of blood appeared around my naturally sharpened nail. I kept pushing and slicing, and soon I opened up what I thought was a sizable incision.

Blood flowed. Languidly, granted, but flowed nonetheless. I positioned the empty juice bottle beneath the cut and caught the first drop of blood as it dripped free. The red stuff flowed free for precisely ten seconds before the wound completely healed. No scar, nothing. Just a dried trail of vampire blood.

I repeated the cutting process, caught the fresh flow of blood, and did this eight more times before I was certain I had enough hemoglobin. Eight cuts, no marks. My arm completely healed.

Yeah, I'm a freak.

I swirled the contents of my blood in the container. A smoothie fit for Satan himself, minus the wheat grass and bee pollen, of course. As I swirled the contents, I thought hard about what I was doing. I even paced the small area in the bathroom and rubbed my neck and debated internally, and in the end, I packed the sealed juice bottle full of my dark plasma into a small Styrofoam container.

I had a friend at the FBI crime lab in D.C. A good friend. I was going to have to trust him, especially if my blood came back...*irregular*. And if it didn't come back irregular? Well, I had nothing to worry about, then, did I?

I'll cross that bridge when I get there.

Most important, I needed answers, and this was the best way I knew of to get them.

I next checked on the packets of Blue Ice that I had stashed in my mini-fridge's mini-freezer an hour or so earlier. The packets were hard as a rock. Good. I placed one under the bottle of blood, one each on either side, and finally one on top. I closed the Styrofoam container, taped it shut, and placed the whole thing in a small cardboard box. I next went online and found the lab's address in D.C. Once done, I placed an order for UPS to swing by the hotel tomorrow morning for a same-day delivery. The same-day delivery was going to cost me $114. I shot off an email to my friend in D.C., telling him to expect a super-sensitive package from yours truly. I ended my email with a smiley face, because I like smiley faces.

When that was taken care of, I switched outfits. I stepped out of my sweats and tee shirt and into something decidedly more slutty. Interestingly, the slutty outfit was something I had borrowed from my sister and never worn.

Anyway, I was now showing more cleavage and shoulder and back, and when I was certain I looked like a skank whore, I grabbed my freshly packed box of blood and my car keys and headed out.

No Wal-Mart run his time.

At the front desk, I dropped off my package and filled in the front desk clerk—whose eyes had bugged out of his head and onto my boobs—to expect UPS tomorrow morning. He nodded distractedly. I wonder what he was distracted about? I made him repeat what I said twice before I headed out.

It was kind of fun being slutty. I think every woman should dress like a slut once in a while. It was very liberating.

Now, acting like a slut was something else entirely.

Maybe that would be liberating, too.

Giggling, I gunned my minivan and headed off to Colton. I had a stripper job to apply for, after all.

Chapter Forty-eight

I parked in the far corner of the dirt parking lot, near where a van was currently a-rocking. I considered a-knocking, just because I hate being told what to do, but ultimately I decided against it, since I really didn't want to know what was going on in there.

And besides, I had a job interview.

Of sorts.

Feeling ridiculous and self-conscious, I strode across the parking lot and up to the front entrance. I didn't see Danny's car, which was a damn good thing.

The bouncer was big and black and scary as hell, even to me. Suddenly insanely self-conscious, I reminded myself that my body still looked like a twenty-eight-year old.

"Excuse me," I said.

"Yeah?" He barely looked at me.

"I hear you're hiring."

He jerked a thumb behind him, toward the inside of the club. "Talk to Rick."

I winked and stepped past him and as I did so, his hand dropped down and grabbed my ass. I convulsed slightly and continued on into the dark club. I entered a small hallway, with an opening at the far end. I passed through the opening and was met by thumping music, losers, and boobs. To my left was the raised stage, which was brightly lit with hundreds of little white light bulbs. The stage was made of dark wood and was heavily scuffed. A single brass pole rose up from the center of the stage, and a single white stripper was currently cavorting around said brass pole. At the moment, just her breasts were out. Her breasts were nothing to write home about, if you ask me. They were fake and probably three or four years past their expiration date. *Don't be catty.* Glitter sparkled between her breasts and over the upper half of her chest. I wondered if any of the men cared about the sparkles. I wondered if any of the men even saw the sparkles.

The place was only half full. Men in varying degrees of drunkenness and physical deterioration sat around the raised stage. Most were drinking beer. Some were drinking shots of the hard stuff. All were staring at the woman with her glittering breasts.

I stood where I was and took in the scene. So why did Danny keep coming here? So what's the draw? Glittering fake breasts?

Maybe. Men have fought for far less.

I continued scanning, realizing I was going to need another hot shower tonight. Smoke filled the air, even though it was illegal to smoke in such establishments. I continued scanning. No one acknowledged me. No one cared that I was standing there at the entrance. A man to my left was currently getting what I assumed was a lap dance, although it looked like a lot of hard grinding. We called that dry humping in my day.

My stomach turned.

Other strippers were making their rounds, running their hands over customer's shoulders and through their hair, offering them some sort of service or another. The men smiled and politely deferred. Many wanted to touch the women, and seemed to forcibly control themselves. Touching the women, I was certain, was highly illegal in such an environment. And, of course, this strip joint was a model in adhering to local laws. *Minus the smoking and the dry humping.* One man actually took a stripper up on her offer, and she promptly led him by the hand into a back room. Another very large man stood outside the door to this room. I shuddered to think what was going on in that back room.

Oh, don't be such a prude, I thought. *It's just sex and lots of it.*

I went over to the bar. A Hispanic bartender was talking to a customer with a thick neck. The bartender didn't look at me. I finally got his attention and told him I wanted to speak to Rick.

The bartender motioned with his jaw, and the customer with the thick neck apparently wasn't a customer at all. The man turned slowly and looked at me. "Waddya want?"

"Are you Rick?"

"Sure."

"I'm looking for a job."

Rick looked me over and somehow held back his excitement. "We ain't hiring, sorry, toots."

Toots? Feeling oddly rejected, I took a gamble. "Danny told me to talk to you about a job."

"Danny, huh?"

"Yeah."

Rick took in a lot of air, which somehow made his thick neck swell out even more. He studied me some more, lingering on my chest. I took in some air and puffed it out a little. Finally, he said, "Come back tonight at eleven when Danny gets here. Then we can all talk to him. But the last I heard, we ain't hiring."

I took another shot in the dark. "But Danny said he was the owner and what he says goes."

"Look, whatever. Come back tonight and we can all have a pow wow." His gaze lingered on me some more. "Let's see your tits and see what we're working with."

I sucked in some air despite myself. I've been undercover before, but not like this. "You can see them tonight, with Danny."

He shrugged and said, "Whatever," and turned back to the bartender, and as I left, I realized that any feelings I had had for Danny, any lingering connection to the man that I had felt, had completely dried up and disappeared in that moment.

Chapter Forty-nine

I was sitting at a Denny's in the city of Corona, drinking a glass of iced water. There was a hot cup of black coffee sitting in front of me, too, but I didn't touch the black coffee. The coffee was there for show, and just to be ordering something.

I idly wondered how many vampires hung out at Denny's. Maybe none. Maybe most vampires were out running through graveyards or having blood orgies, or whatever the hell else real vampires do.

The waitress came by and glanced at my full cup of coffee and asked if I needed anything else. I smiled and said no. She smiled and dropped off the check and left. I smiled just for the hell of it.

I had a notebook in front of me, open to a blank page. I was loosely holding a pen near the top of the blank page. As I sat there, I remembered the grounding steps from last time, and performed them now. In my mind's eye, I saw myself securely tethered to the earth with glowing silver cords. Then I took in some air and held it for a few minutes and then let it out slowly.

A now familiar tingling appeared in my arm. The pen jerked in my hands. It jerked again, and now the tip was moving, writing. Three words appeared.

Good evening, Samantha.

I stared at them, knowing I should probably be freaked out, but I wasn't. Whatever the hell was going on, I didn't know, but I was game to go along for the ride.

I spoke by subvocalizing the words, that is, speaking them with barely a whisper, just loud enough for me to hear, and hopefully loud enough for my new friend to hear. But, of course, not so loud that I would get thrown out of Denny's.

"Good evening, Sephora," I said. "How are you?"

I'm well. And I can hear you just fine.

I smiled. "I'm sorry I haven't gotten back to you earlier."

There is no reason to feel sorry, Samantha. Remember, I'm always here.

"Yes, you said that. And where is here?"

Where do you think it is?

"Heaven?"

Close. Let's call it the 'spirit world'.

"And what's that like, the spirit world?"

Oh, you know it well.

"I do?"

Indeed, a very significant part of you still resides in the spirit world.

"You totally lost me."

You are much more than your physical body, Samantha. Do you understand the concept of a soul?

"Yes. I just don't know if I believe in the concept of a soul."

I understand. You live in this physical world of time and space. There isn't, admittedly, a lot of evidence of a soul. Then again, there isn't a lot of evidence for vampires, either. But both exist.

I nodded and sipped my ice water. The coffee had quit letting off steam. Quickly, when no one was looking, I poured a little out onto the table and then mopped it up with my napkin. Now the coffee at least appeared to have been sipped. I wrapped another napkin around the sopping wet napkin. The things I do to appear normal. Sigh.

"So some things are taken on faith, is that what you're saying?"

Something like that, Samantha.

"You can call me Sam."

I'll do that...Sam.

"So what did you mean that a significant part of me still resides in the spirit world?"

The easiest way to describe this, Sam, is to say that not all of your soul is focused in your current physical body. Some of your soul—a large portion of your soul, in fact—still resides in the spirit world.

"And what's it doing in the spirit world?"

Watching you, closely.

"This is a lot to take," I said. "And weird."

I understand. So take things slowly. There's time. There's no rush.

"And who are you, exactly?"

Just a friend, Sam.

"A good friend?"

The best.

"Okay, that makes me feel better," I said, and as I said those words quietly, I felt a slight shiver course along the entire length of my body. Oddly, it was a comforting sensation. There was a good chance I might have just been hugged.

I'm glad you feel better, Sam.

"I want to ask you more about me, about what I have become, but maybe that can wait until another night."

I'm always here, Sam.

And just like that, the electrified sensation left my body. I closed the notebook, put the pen back in my purse (along with the sopping napkin, which I had wrapped another napkin around), and paid my bill and left.

Chapter Fifty

The more I thought about delivering Orange County's most notorious crime boss into the hands of the mild mannered Stuart Young, the more I realized I had given my perfectly bald client a death sentence.

And so I spent a lot of that night thinking about what I could do about this dilemma. I thought long and hard, and somewhere near the break of dawn, I came up with an idea.

***

I spent all the next evening researching the plane crash; in particular, the victims on board. Because this was a military crash and because most of the victims were key witnesses to an important trial, getting the names wasn't easy. I used every available contact I had in the federal government until finally a list was provided to me.

And once I had the list I went to work.

***

Two days later, on the night of the full moon, with Kingsley howling away deep inside his safe room—I hoped—I alighted on Jerry Blum's wonderfully ornate alabaster balcony.

I tucked in my massive, leathery wings, focused my thoughts on the woman in the dancing flame, opened my eyes, and found myself standing naked on his stone balcony.

Naked but not without a plan.

My talons might be hideous and scary as hell, but they were good at carrying smaller objects. And one of them, this time, had been my daughter's extra backpack. The backpack was full of, let's just say, crime fighting gear.

Below me, I heard the muted sounds of men talking quietly among themselves. So far, I hadn't been seen. The sliding glass door in front of me was wide open. Apparently, Jerry Blum never expected a giant vampire bat to alight on his balcony. From within the room, I heard the sounds of muffled snoring.

I stepped into his darkened bedroom. My eyes did not need adjusting. His spacious room was electrified with shining filaments of zigzagging light. Ghost light. Vampire light. There was a lone figure sleeping in a massive four poster bed. White gossamer sheets hung from the bed's cross beams. Very *un*crime lord-like.

The figure sleeping in the center of the bed was snoring softly, peacefully, contentedly. There was no evidence that this son-of-bitch stayed awake over the crimes against humanity he had committed.

There was a white cotton robe hanging over the wooden sleigh bed footboard. I slipped it on and assessed the situation. I was certain there were guards somewhere nearby, although none seemed directly outside the door. I didn't hear them, nor was my sixth sense jangling. My sixth sense was telling me that, for now, I was safe.

Carrying the backpack, I went over to the side of the bed and looked down at the man who had presumably killed Stuart's wife, a man who was powerful enough to bring down a government-owned airplane. There was a reason why I didn't confront him directly and openly. He would have gone after me and everything I loved, too. I had to hunt him from afar.

I had another reason for being here. Before I condemned the man to death, I had to know if I had the right man. Sure, Jerry Blum was a bastard. But was he the bastard I wanted?

Well, let's find out.

"Wake up, asshole," I said.

Jerry Blum's eyes popped open instantly. His hand snaked beneath his pillow, a practiced motion. He was fast, but I was faster. In a blink, his arm was pinned up over his head, driven into the mattress by my own hand, and I found myself leaning over him, staring down into his startled face. It was a face I had seen often: in the news, in books, and even in magazines. He was a celebrity crime lord, if ever there was one. Celebrity or not, he was a son-of-a-bitch. He was also quite handsome. Blum was in his late fifties, but he could have passed for his early forties. There was some gray at his temples, and there were fine lines that creased from the corners of his eyes and reached down to the corners of his mouth. These were not laugh lines. Worry lines, no doubt. Jerry Blum was not a big man, but I could feel his muscular body beneath me. Shockingly, amazingly, I found myself slightly turned on by the position I found myself in: pinning down a handsome devil in his bed in the middle of the night.

I shook off the feeling as soon as it registered.

He quit struggling, perhaps realizing it was doing him no good, and we stared at each other for a heartbeat or two. Ambient light made its way in through the open French doors. Laughter reached us from somewhere on his grounds, but not very close. A girl giggled. An airplane droned high overhead.

Jerry Blum had thin lips. Too thin for me. He breathed easily, his nostrils flaring slightly. He smelled of good cologne and something else. Lavender. But the scent wasn't coming from him. It was coming from his bed; in fact, it was coming from his pillow. I knew something about aromatherapy. One sprinkled lavender on one's pillow to ensure a good night's sleep. No doubt Mr. Blum had been plagued by a lifetime of nightmares. Or not.

"Who the fuck are you?" he finally said.

"Your worst nightmare," I said, and somehow managed to keep a straight face.

"Yeah, well, you look like a whore."

He next tried to throw me off. *Tried* being the operative word here. He grunted and grimaced and bucked, but I didn't go anywhere. Finally, he lay back, gasping, face contorted slightly in pain. I think he might have pulled something.

"You're a very bad man, Mr. Blum."

"And you're a dead woman."

"You're closer than you think," I said.

He opened his mouth to yell or scream and I used my other hand to slap his face hard. It was a nice slap, harder than I intended, but I didn't care. His eyes literally crossed, then settled back into place. A moment later, he was staring up at me in a daze.

"No yelling or screaming," I said.

Blood trickled from the corner of his mouth. My stomach lurched. I purposely had not eaten tonight.

"Did Danny Boy send you up?"

"No."

"So you ain't no whore?"

"That's a double negative, Mr. Blum."

"What the fuck is going on?"

I found myself staring down at the fine trickle of

blood that glistened at the corner of his mouth. Blood was food for me, sure, but it was also something else. The right blood—fresh blood—satisfied more than hunger.

I said, "Do you want the bad news, Jerry, or the really bad news?"

He fought me again, this time harder than before, doing his damnedest to buck me off him. But I didn't move, and he quickly tired of this game, gasping. And that's when I punched him. Hard. It was a straight jab into his left eye. I put a lot of strength behind the punch. I wanted it to hurt. The sound of bone hitting bone was sickening, and the punch drove his head deep into the pillow, where the goose down bloomed around him like a white flower, no doubt dousing him in peaceful lavender.

A very small voice protested what I was doing, as it had been doing all night long. It reminded me that I was a mother, a sister, a friend, an ex-federal agent, an ex-wife, a woman with a conscience and a heart. It reminded me that I was not a killer or a murderer.

And as Jerry Blum shook his head, as a deep cut along the edge of his orbital ridge dripped blood into the corner of his left eye, I listened to that voice. I listened to its arguments and I listened to its reasoning, and I decided, in the end, that Jerry Blum had to die.

But not yet. First, I needed information. First, I had to know.

I said, "You sabotaged an airplane carrying a half dozen government witnesses. The airplane crashed killing everyone on board."

"I don't know what you're talking about."

I punched him again, harder than before, driving his head deeper into the pillow.

"Fuck," he said. Blood was now staining his pillowcase, no doubt adding a nice coppery smell to the lavender.

I didn't come here to beat up Jerry Blum. I didn't come here to intimidate him. I came here to get a confession from him. And what happened after that, well, I was going to play that by ear.

"Tell me about the plane, Jerry," I said.

"Do you have any idea who I am?"

"You're Jerry Blum. Orange County's biggest crime lord. You are untouchable. Your enemies shudder in your presence. You've destroyed lives and businesses and spread fear far and wide. Did I miss anything?"

"Yeah, I'm rich. I can triple whoever's paying."

"Paying me to do what?"

"To kill me."

"They didn't pay me to kill you, Mr. Blum. I tossed that in as a freebie. Pro bono, so to speak."

He lay back in his bed, bleeding. His nose was perfect, probably surgically altered. His teeth were perfect, probably dentally enhanced. He let out a long breath. His breath was tinged with the scent of blood. In fact, blood wafted up from him everywhere. He wasn't bleeding a lot, granted, but a little bit of blood registered deeply with me.

I'm a shark, I thought, *smelling blood in the water dozens of miles away.*

"Tell me about the plane," I said. The blood, quite honestly, was driving me fucking crazy.

"Go to hell, cunt."

"Tell me about the plane, Jerry."

He threw his face at me, lips pulled back, cords standing out on his neck. His eyes veritably bulged from their sockets. He fought and fought and screeched in frustration and anger and pain, and when he spoke spittle shot from his mouth in a steady stream. "Of course I killed them, you fucking freaky bitch! Just like I'm going to kill you. You can't stop me, no one can stop me. I'm invincible. I kill who I want, when I want, and how I want. You understand, you crazy bitch? You understand? You're a dead woman. Dead! And so is your client and anyone else you fucking know! And that's after I fuck you every which way, you fucking whore! How dare you come into my house, how dare you come in here and—"

And that's as far as he got.

"Enough," I said.

I flipped Jerry Blum over and pulled his hands behind his back. I reached into my bag of tricks and pulled out a pair of handcuffs. I cuffed the bastard and then pulled a black, breathable hood over his face. I cinched it tight. He fought me like a demon on crack, bucking and twisting, but it did him no good.

When I was finished, I hauled him to his feet and threw him over my shoulder. I carried him to his beautiful alabaster balcony, where I set him down, along with my backpack, and ditched the robe. I closed my eyes and saw the flame and the hulking winged creature. When I opened my eyes again, I was easily five feet taller than I had been just seconds before. Jerry was still pinned beneath me, this time beneath one of my massive talons.

My hands in this form are quite dextrous; unfortunately, they're also attached to my wings, just like a bat. Still, I used my hands to drape the backpack over one of my talons. Once done, I gripped Jerry Blum by his shoulders. No doubt my claws hurt like hell.

I flapped my wings hard, causing a thunderous downdraft that whipped Jerry's hair crazily. He screamed and fought me some more, but had no clue what was happening to him. And as I got a little air under me, I adjusted my grip on the crime lord, using both talons now. I flapped my wings harder and now I was rising up into the night sky, Blum dangling beneath me like a kangaroo rat.

Chapter Fifty-one

We were in the predetermined clearing in Carbon Canyon. One of us unwillingly.

Still wearing the black hood, Jerry Blum was handcuffed to a tree branch, his hands high above him. He had cussed and hollered the entire twenty minute flight here. I flew on, ignoring him, catching a high altitude current that made flapping my wings a breeze. Once we had arrived in the clearing, I had transformed again and slipped into a little black dress that I had included in my bag of tricks. Blum was full of questions and vitriol and hate. I ignored all of his questions as I cuffed him to the tree branch.

Now from my bag of tricks, I removed my cell phone. I selected eleven recipients and sent out a single text message. I next made a call to my client, Stuart Young. In so many words, I told Stuart that the eagle had landed. I had our man. Stuart had paused, swallowed hard, and said he would be here as soon as possible.

I left Jerry Blum alone, secured to the tree. Jerry Blum, as far as I was concerned, had dug his own grave. From my backpack, I fished out a pack of cigarettes and fired one up and inhaled deeply. I had stepped out of the clearing and into a thicket of twisted trees. As I exhaled, I looked up at the full moon, now just a silver mosaic through the tangle of branches. My thoughts were empty. My heart was empty. I felt empty and cold. I listened to the sounds the forest made, and the sounds of my own distant beating heart. I finished the cigarette and immediately lit another just to be doing something. Jerry Blum bellowed angrily from the clearing behind me, but I ignored him. *He dug his own grave.* I finished the second cigarette but decided against a third. I finally leaned a shoulder against a dusty tree trunk and closed my eyes and stayed in that position until I heard the crunch of tires from somewhere nearby.

***

I met Stuart on the dirt road, about a hundred yards away from the clearing. Stuart did not look good. He looked sick and scared and probably had to go to the bathroom.

"I have to go to the bathroom," he said.

I nodded and he dashed off. A moment later, he

came back, zipping up. He said, "So he's really here?"

I nodded, watching him. "Yes."

"I want to see him."

I nodded again and led Stuart through the forest and into the clearing, which was dappled in bright moonlight. Jerry Blum heard us coming and raised his head.

Seeing a man chained to a tree was no doubt unnerving to Stuart. He immediately stopped in his tracks. "Oh, my God."

Blum shouted, "Who's there, goddammit?"

I ignored Blum. Instead, I took Stuart's hand and walked him over to the shackled crime lord. I removed the hood and Blum shook his head and squinted. I handed Stuart a flashlight from the backpack and he clicked it on and shined it straight into Blum's face, who turned away, blinking hard and spitting mad.

"Goddammit! Who the fuck are you two? What the fuck is going on? How the fuck did I get here?"

"Shut the fuck up, Jerry," I said.

"Fuck you, cunt." He spit at me, tried to kick me. He succeeded in only losing his footing and hanging briefly by the cuffs.

Stuart said nothing. He simply stared in open-mouthed wonder at the man hanging from the tree. Still open-mouthed, Stuart then turned to me.

"You really did it," he said.

I said nothing. I was watching Stuart. My client still did not look good. He looked, in fact, a little hysterical. I covered Jerry's head again and led Stuart away. Blum screamed and repeatedly threw his body against the tree trunk. Stuart looked back but I pulled him along through the high grass to the far end of the clearing. Once there, we stopped.

"And no one knows he's here?"

"No one who matters."

Stuart nodded. His wild eyes were looking increasingly erratic.

"Are you okay?" I asked Stuart.

"I don't know if I can do this, Sam."

"I understand."

Stuart was shaking. He ran a hand over his bald head. "I hate him so much, so fucking much. I still can't believe he's here. How did you do it?"

I shook my head; Stuart nodded. The wind picked up considerably, swishing the branches along the edge of the clearing and slapping the tall grass around our ankles.

And through the wind, I heard many more vehicles driving up along the dirt road. One after another. Stuart didn't hear them. Stuart was lost in his own thoughts. Stuart also didn't have my hearing.

"You don't have to do this," I said.

Stuart nodded. Tears were in his eyes.

"I hate him so fucking much."

We were silent some more. The wind continued to pick up, moaning through the trees. I heard footsteps coming. Many footsteps.

I said, "What if I told you that you didn't have

to do this alone, Stuart?"

"What do you mean?"

"What if I told you that Jerry Blum had wronged many people the day he killed your wife? What if I told you that many, many people share your desire for revenge."

"I don't understand."

I waved my hand and in that moment ten figures stepped out of the woods. Ten solemn, white-faced figures. I recognized the faces, all of whom I had met in the past few days. All of whom I had easily convinced to be here tonight. Not one needed prodding. All had jumped at the opportunity.

"Jerry Blum is a bad man, Stuart. He would have hurt you tonight. He would have killed you."

"Who are they?"

"People like you, Stuart, all victims of Jerry Blum."

"What's going to happen tonight?"

"I don't know," I said. "I'm leaving that to all of you."

Stuart looked at me with impossibly wide eyes. He then looked at the others, most of whom nodded at him. They were all here. Mothers, wives, husbands, and children. All had lost loved ones in the crash.

I squeezed Stuart's hand and then left him there with the others. I went over to Jerry Blum and uncuffed him. I took his blindfold off and led him over to the center of the clearing.

"Who the fuck are those assholes?" said Jerry.

He only fought me a little.

I didn't answer him. Instead, I turned and walked away, leaving Jerry alone in the light of the full moon. Off to the side of the clearing, I quickly slipped out of the dress and shoved my cell and cuffs and keys inside the backpack.

I had just transformed when I heard the first gunshot. And as I leaped high into the air and flapped my wings hard and flew away from the isolated canyon, I heard shot after shot after shot.

***

I asked Stuart a few days later what had happened on the night of the full moon, but he wouldn't give me an answer. And neither would the others.

I had been wrong about Jerry Blum. He didn't dig his own grave. I very much suspected the others had done it for him, leaving Orange County's notorious crime lord buried deep in that forgotten clearing.

Chapter Fifty-two

I don't get exhausted, but I get mentally fatigued, and tonight had stretched me thin. I was looking forward to coming home to my empty hotel room, closing the curtains tight, and sleeping the day away, dead to the world.

But as I unlocked the door to my room with the keycard and stepped inside, I was immediately met by two things: the first was a fresh breeze that was blowing in through my wide open balcony door, and the second was a nearly overwhelmingly foul stench.

Last time I had been surprised in such a fashion, a vampire hunter had been waiting for me. And what was waiting for me now, stunned even me.

***

Alert for silver-tipped arrows or silver ninja stars or silver anything else hurling at me, I cautiously entered my hotel room.

I moved cautiously down the very small hallway. To my left was a closet. The door was partially open. I knew immediately there was no one inside. No, whoever was in my suite was in my living room or sleeping area.

The lights were out. Squiggly, rapidly-moving prisms of light shot wildly through the air. These super-charged particles of light illuminated my way, as they always did.

I took another step into my suite.

I was approaching the end of the short hallway. Around the corner to the right would be my bed and the desk. Around the corner to my left were sitting chairs and a round table. Presently, from my position, I could not see very far around either corner.

Directly before me, at the far end of my suite, I could see the sliding glass door. Or what had once been the sliding glass door, as most of the glass was presently scattered across the carpet. The heavy curtains shifted in the breeze, swaying slightly.

I took another step.

My sixth sense was buzzing. The fine hairs on my neck were standing on end. The foul stench grew stronger. Something rancid was in my hotel room.

No, something *dead* was in my room.

I took another step. I was now at the end of the

hallway. To my right, I could see the foot of the bed. To my left, was a section of the round table. The stench, I was certain, was coming from my right, on the side where my bed and desk were located.

I paused, listening.

Someone was breathing around the corner. Deep breaths, ragged breaths. My heart thumped fast and hard. I suddenly wished I had a weapon.

You are a weapon, I reminded myself.

I continued listening to the breathing. A slow sound. A deep sound. A rumbling sound. Something big was in my living room. Either that or someone parked a Dodge Charger on my bed.

I stepped around the corner.

***

The thing standing in the corner of my room was horrific and nightmarish, and if I wasn't so terrified, I would have turned and ran or peed myself. Instead, I stopped and stared and still might have peed myself a little.

The thing was watching me closely, almost curiously, its head slightly angled, its pointed ears erect and alert. Its lower face—or muzzle—projected out slightly, but not quite as long as a traditional dog, or wolf. More like a pug.

Standing there in the corner of my room, the thing looked like a long-forgotten Hollywood movie prop.

Except this movie prop was breathing deeply and growling just under its breath. A low growl. A warning growl. The same kind of growl a guard dog would give. Except this growl was terrifyingly deep.

Blood was dripping from its face. Blood, and something else. Something blackish. Something putrid. I suddenly had a very strong sense that it had dug up a body and feasted on it. In fact, I was certain of this. How I was certain of it, I didn't know. Maybe my sixth sense was evolving into something more.

Or maybe because this thing smells like the walking dead.

I made sure my back was to the open glass door. I wasn't sure what I would do if the thing attacked, but having a readily available escape route seemed like a damned good idea. And if I had to take flight, well, I could kiss these clothes goodbye. They would burst from my body in an instant.

A part of me felt like this was a dream. Hell, *a lot* of me felt like this was a dream.

We continued staring at each other. I continued wanting to pee. The creature continued breathing deeply, throatily. I could have been standing next to a tiger cage.

And that's when the beast took a step toward me.

Every instinct told me to run—and to keep running until I had put hundreds of miles between me and this *thing*. But I didn't run. Something kept me in that room. That something was curiosity.

Curiosity killed the cat. Or, in this case, the vampire.

It took another step toward me. A very long step. One that spanned nearly the entire length of my bed. As it walked, it sort of tucked in its shaggy elbows.

The thing, I was certain, was a werewolf. And that werewolf, I was certain, was Kingsley.

When I transformed, I was all there; meaning, I was still me, and I could control all of my actions and emotions. I doubted Kingsley would have chosen to dig up a grave and feast upon a corpse, if that was, in fact, what he had done. So that alone suggested Kingsley was not all here. Meaning, something else was controlling this beast. But enough of Kingsley was in there to find his way to my hotel room tonight.

What happened to the panic room? And where was Franklin the Butler who, I knew, looked after Kingsley during these monthly transformations?

You ask a lot of questions, vampire.

The words appeared in my thoughts, directly inside my skull, as if someone had whispered them straight into my ear cavity. I didn't jump, but I did step back.

"Who said that?"

As I spoke, the creature cocked its head to one side, its pointed ears, moving independently of each other, shot forward. Cute on a dog, not so cute on a hulking, nightmarish creature.

Who do you think said it, vampire?

The creature stepped forward. Its movements were graceful and surprisingly economical. It only moved when it had to. Nothing wasted.

"Kingsley?" I asked.

Kingsley's not home.

"Then who is this?"

The werewolf stepped closer still, and the wave of revulsion that emanated from it nearly made me retch.

I reminded myself that I was a terrifying creature of the night, able to strike fear in the hearts of even the most hardened criminals.

You look afraid, vampire, said the voice in my head.

Up close, the creature looked even more hideous. And up close, it smelled even worse.

"Who are you?" I asked again. My voice shook.

Does it matter?

"Yes. I want to know where my friend is."

Oh, he's in here, vampire.

"Where is here?"

In the background, vampire. Watching us.

Moonlight reflected off the creature's thick brow and slightly protruding muzzle. Long, white teeth gleamed over black gums. A low, steady, rumble came from its throat and chest. The creature seemed incapable of remaining silent. A low growl seemed to continuously emanate from it. I fought a nearly overwhelming desire to step back. But I didn't.

You are brave, vampire.

"And you smell like shit."

The werewolf tilted its head. One of its ears revolved out to the side, hearing something that was beyond even my own keen hearing.

Kingsley has been wanting to see you, vampire. Very badly. But he has refused to do so out of pride. But I thought I would take it upon myself to visit you tonight. I thought it was time to make your acquaintance. There are, after all, so few of us.

"Us?"

The undead.

"Fine, so you've met me. Now who the fuck are you?"

The werewolf growled a deeper growl, a sound which seemed to resonate from deep within its massive chest.

I am called Maltheus.

I did my best to wrap my brain around what I was hearing. "You are a separate entity that lives within Kingsley?"

Not always within, no. But I do visit him once a month. He's such a gracious host.

I sensed sarcasm. "And what, exactly, are you?"

I am many things, vampire.

"How is it that you can take possession of Kingsley? How is that you can turn into this thing?"

This thing, as you call it, is my physical incarnation. And I took possession of my dear fellow Kingsley because he allowed me inside him.

"He *wanted* to be bitten by a werewolf?"

No. He wanted death. He wanted revenge. He was full of hate and despair and emptiness. The voice paused; the werewolf stared down at me, breathing heavily through a partially open mouth. Its lips were pure black. *I exist to fill that emptiness.*

"I don't understand."

You will someday, vampire. And we will meet again. Of that, you can be sure.

In a blink of an eye, moving faster than any creature that size had a right to move, the werewolf turned its massive shoulders and dashed through the shattered door and leaped off the stucco balcony.

I ran over to the edge and watched as it dropped nine stories, landing softly and gracefully. It didn't throw back its head and let loose with an ear-splitting howl, nor did it dash off into the night on all four legs.

No, it simply sniffed the air, scratched behind its ear, and walked calmly away.

Chapter Fifty-three

It was late and my IM chat window was open. So far, there was no sign of Fang.

I had spent the past three hours cleaning my room, picking up glass and scrubbing clean the blood and other bodily fluids that had been dripping from Kingsley. With the place clean, now all I had to do was come up with a convincing story about the broken glass. I decided on going the drunken, divorced mother route. I had been drinking on the balcony, when I stumbled through the glass door. Could happen to anyone.

Now, with my hotel suite smelling like coconut butter and rotted corpse, I was sitting in front of my computer, waiting for Fang to log on.

I buzzed him again.

And again.

Twenty minutes later, I saw what I wanted to see: a flashing pencil had appeared in the message box. Fang was writing me a message. I felt overjoyed and relieved. I had come to rely on Fang more than he realized.

More than *I* realized.

A moment later, his words appeared: *You are persistent tonight, Moon Dance.*

I have news.

Of that, I have no doubt.

Were you asleep?

I might have been dozing, but I always have time for you, Moon Dance.

My heart swelled. *Thank you, Fang.*

He typed a smiley face and then asked: *So what's your news?*

I saw a werewolf tonight.

Your old client and new lover?

I hesitated. *Yes.*

Tell me about it.

And so I did. I relayed everything that had happened and what was said to the best of my ability. As I typed, Fang waited patiently. Then again, he might have fallen back to sleep.

Nope. I had barely sent my message, when his response appeared nearly instantly.

I'm not surprised. It is commonly believed that werewolves feast on corpses.

Well, if he thinks he's ever going to kiss me with those ghoulish lips again, he's got another think coming.

Isn't that a bit like the teapot calling the kettle black?

I don't eat corpses, Fang.

Point taken. So you say this entity claimed to be living inside your friend?

Yes, I wrote.

Fang paused, then wrote: *There are some who believe that werewolves and other such creatures of the night are, in fact, the physical manifestations of highly evolved dark masters.*

I'm not sure I'm following.

These beings, these powerful entities, are forbidden to incarnate on earth. But they have found, let's call them, loopholes.

And one such loophole is to incarnate once a month, as werewolves.

Exactly. But they don't consider themselves wolves. You are, in fact, looking at the physical expression of the darkest of evils.

I shuddered.

And how do they find...a host?

No doubt the usual ways. Being bitten by such a being would be one way. But generally, and I think your ex-client is proof of this, they attach themselves to a willing host.

I'm lost, I wrote. *As usual.*

I have no doubt that your ex-client, the attorney, did not pointedly ask to be a werewolf. But he projected weakness, anguish, pain, despair. Such extreme emotions attract the attention of these highly evolved dark masters. It was just a matter of time until a werewolf-like creature found its way to your friend. Either that, or death.

So they saw my friend as a good host.

You could say that.

So, in effect, he is possessed.

Exactly. But he's possessed by something very dark, and very, very evil.

The sun will be up soon, I wrote.

Spoken like a true vampire. So are we still on for Sunday night?

That was two days from now. My heart slammed in my chest. *Yes.*

Where would you like to meet, Moon Dance?

You are in Southern California? I asked.

Yes.

Are you familiar with Orange County?

Yes.

Do you know where the Downtown Grill is in Fullerton?

There was a pause. *Yes.*

Okay, I will see you there at midnight.

The vampire's hour. So midnight it is, Moon Dance.

Goodnight, Fang.

You mean good morning.

Ha-ha.

Sweet dreams, Moon Dance. See you soon.

Chapter Fifty-four

I got up earlier than normal to take care of the sliding glass door with hotel management.

Groggy, weak, and feeling less than human, I walked the short, stocky and highly disapproving woman through my fictional drunken escapade last night, which culminated in me supposedly crashing through the glass door. She clucked her tongue numerous times, and in the end, after taking a few photographs of the damages, she seemed to buy my story. An hour or so later, a work crew stopped by and replaced the glass.

As they worked, I wondered if it was finally time for me to find my own place. Of course, I already had my own place. It was the house Danny and I had purchased together. The house he was currently using to fuck his secretary in.

I had been at the Embassy Suites for two

months now. Surely, it was time for a change. And with that thought in mind, as I sat in the center of my bed while the work crew positioned the big piece of glass in the balcony doorway, I realized what I *hadn't* seen in the seedy strip club in Colton.

Heart pounding, I fired up my laptop. I jacked into the hotel wireless service and did a quick search for the club. As I expected, there was no mention of it. No mention of it, in fact, anywhere.

As the work crew finished, one of them suggested that next time I fall *away* from the glass door when I was shit-faced drunk. I told him I would keep his suggestion in mind (asshole), and when they were gone, so was I.

Covered in sunscreen and heavy clothing, sporting my cool sunhat and shades, I grabbed my keys and hit the road.

***

Along the way to the Riverside County Courthouse, my cell phone rang. It was Kingsley. I picked up immediately.

"Hey," he said.

"Hey."

"I'm sorry about last night," he said.

"Last night was a little terrifying. At least I no longer doubt that you really are a...you know what."

Kingsley hated for us to talk about our super secret identities on the phone. He actually laughed. "This coming from a...you know what."

"We all have our hang ups."

He was silent as I drove along the congested freeway. Mercifully, the sun was behind me.

Finally, Kingsley said, "Am I to understand you took care of my client the other night?"

"You are to understand anything you want."

I could almost see him nod. "I should be very pissed off at you for that."

"You should thank me. I lessened your workload."

"That was very reckless, Sam."

"These are reckless times."

He was silent some more. I suspected he was in his massive office, surrounded by piles of files.

"So what do we do, Sam?"

"About what?"

"About us."

"I don't know," I said.

"I like you. A lot."

"I'm a very likable person," I said.

He chuckled. "Sometimes. But now you're being distant and cold."

"I feel distant and cold, so no surprise there."

"It's because of what I do," he said.

"I hate what you do."

"Sometimes I help people, Sam. Not everyone belongs in prison."

"And not everyone should be freed on a technicality."

"We can argue this forever," he said.

"And forever is a very long time for...us."

He chuckled lightly again. "Can I see you tomorrow night?"

"Tomorrow night I have plans."

He made a noise on the phone. I know he wanted to ask who my plans were with but he held back. "I see. Perhaps next week?"

"Perhaps," I said.

"I'll call you later."

I said okay and we hung up.

***

My cell rang again. I checked the number and ID on the faceplate. The number came up "Restricted". It was either a creditor or one of my pals with law enforcement. My finances had gotten a little out of hand these past few months. My hotel room hadn't been cheap and Danny wasn't helping me. I took my chances and clicked on.

"I don't have any money," I said.

"Hello? Sam, it's Mel."

Oops. It was my DNA biologist friend from the FBI Crime Lab. Definitely not a creditor, although he did accept deposits in blood. My heart immediately slammed hard against the inside of my ribs. His call could only mean one thing.

"What's shaking, Mel?"

"I have the results to your blood work up, Sam."

I took a deep breath, held it, and then said, "Okay. Lay them on me."

Chapter Fifty-five

Danny's firm took up the entire second floor of the office building. The building itself wasn't much to write home about. Squarish and ugly and immediately forgotten. A couple of years ago, I had jokingly referred to the building as "Ambulance Chaser Headquarters", and Danny had refused to speak to me for two days.

The big baby.

With the sun still a few hours from setting and myself not at my strongest, I climbed the exterior stairs and pushed through the smoky glass doors. Four leather chairs sat empty to one side of the door. A thick, square mohair carpet spanned the length of the office. A bubbling fountain gurgled in the corner to my left, projecting an aura of zen-like calm in these troubled, accident-prone times. On the walls were the paintings I had picked out with

Danny at a swap meet years ago. Big, fake, cheap stuff.

And directly in front of me, sitting behind a kidney-shaped desk, with her shiny, tan legs crossed and absently texting on her cell phone, was my ex-husband's new secretary. The woman he had cheated on me with. The woman he was currently fucking. The woman he entertained at our house, in our bedroom, in our bed. The woman he had introduced to our children.

She had known that he was married. No doubt he had made me out to be a monster. No doubt he had painted a picture of an unfit mother. Unfit or not, she had chosen to cheat with a married man. My married man.

She set her phone aside, uncrossed her thin legs, and gave me a big smile. She was about to ask if she could help me, but then stopped short. Her mouth sort of hung open and her eyes narrowed. She was an ugly woman, I thought. I had no clue what Danny saw in her. Face too thin, skin too tan, boobs too fake. On second thought, I saw exactly what Danny saw in her. She was the opposite of me.

She jumped up and moved quickly around her desk, blocking my path. She crossed her arms under her fake breasts. Her nails were red and long. She looked like a whore.

"What the fuck are you doing here?" she said.

I smiled and, without breaking stride, punched her straight in the face. She flew backward, bounced off the desk, spun around and landed on her face.

On her nose, in fact. She moaned. I wasn't at full strength and I certainly didn't hit her as hard as I could, but she would remember me.

Danny appeared from his office door, open-mouthed. He looked at me and then at his secretary on the mohair rug. "Sam, what the fuck is going on?"

And as he stepped out of the office, I punched him hard in his stomach. He *oofed* nicely and doubled over. I grabbed him by the collar and threw him back into his office and shut the door behind me.

Chapter Fifty-six

I pushed him down into one of his leather client chairs and sat on the edge of his executive desk, which was big enough to land an F-17 on.

Danny still hadn't gotten his breath back entirely. His face was purplish and contorted, and he was staring at me with frightened, angry eyes.

I kicked my legs pleasantly and whistled absently, waiting for his lungs to kick start again. Finally his short rasping breaths turned into longer rasping breaths. And when they did, words vomited from his mouth. "What the fuck are...who the hell do you...you have royally fucked yourself...how dare you attack...."

"Are you quite done, asshole?"

He sat up straighter, took in a long, agonized breath. "I demand to know what's going on."

"Well, since you asked so nicely."

I grinned and continued swinging my legs. I shouldn't have been enjoying this so much, but I was.

He looked at me with very confused, very dark eyes. Danny was not a big guy. Just a few inches shy of six foot, he was also too skinny for me, but I never told him that. I had always liked my men a little beefier, which is why Kingsley had been so damn intoxicating.

He said, "Do you have any idea the shit you just landed yourself in, Sam?"

"About as much shit as you landed in, dickhead."

His eyes narrowed. "What the hell does that mean?"

There was a low moan from outside the closed door, followed by some sobbing. His secretary lying there on the carpet, crying, probably wasn't good for business.

"You're the owner of The Kittycat," I said. "Perhaps the world's sleaziest strip club. In fact, you're the sole owner of it."

The color drained from his already pale face. He tried to sit up. I told him to stay where he was and he did so.

"I don't know what you're talking about, Sam."

"Of course you don't. Deny everything, right? It's the losers' motto."

"Sam, you're talking nonsense."

"Am I? All I have to do is make one call to any number of my friends in law enforcement, and they will come down hard on The Kittycat."

"Just wait a second, Sam. Whether or not I own the business is beside the point. It's hardly a crime to run a strip club."

I crossed my arms under my chest. My own natural bosom didn't push up unnaturally through the top of my own blouse and I was proud of that.

"It's a crime, Danny, when said business—in particular, a *strip club*—operates without a license."

"Shit."

I grinned and sat back. I swung my legs some more. Seeing Danny squirm had just become my favorite new hobby.

"I'm in the process of getting a license—"

"*In the process of* and *having one* are two different things, Danny. And you know that. But you couldn't wait, could you? You just had to open the doors to that shithole of sleaze."

He said nothing. I could see his pressed shirt pulsating slightly over his hammering heart. His mind was spinning in ten different directions. But there was no getting out of this one. Not for him.

"What the fuck happened to you, Danny?" I asked. "How does a respectable family man end up owning that dungeon of filth?"

"I don't have to answer you."

"Hey, I'm not the cops, Danny boy. There are no Miranda rights and I'm not wired. This is just between you and me."

"Well, you don't know what the fuck you're talking about. Now, can I check on Sugar?"

I laughed into my hand. "Sugar?"

"Not now, Sam—"

"Her name is Sugar? Honest to God? Is she also one of your filthy strippers, Danny? Sucking up to the boss in more ways than one?"

"Okay, you caught me. So sue me for looking outside of our shitty marriage for something more. So sue me for jumping on a chance to own something that's going to make me a lot of money."

"You're pathetic."

"And you're a living nightmare. What the fuck do you want, Sam?"

I studied him long and hard. Sugar had quit sobbing from the other side of the door. Sugar wasn't happy.

I said, "I want the house and I want the kids."

He laughed. "No way. There is absolutely no fucking way I'm letting you around our kids unsupervised."

"I don't think you understand the quagmire of shit you find yourself in, Danny. If I say the word, the hammer comes down on your disgusting enterprise. You're looking at an ungodly amount of fines, not to mention automatic disbarment. Oh, yeah, and the world will see you as the slimeball you've turned out to be. And I can't wait to see what your mother thinks about all of this, too." I paused, shaking my head. "No one stops to consider their mothers. It's a pity."

"You forget, Sam. If you say anything, I will expose you for the monster you really are."

I slipped off the desk and approached him slowly. I squatted down between his legs, resting my elbows on his knees. He was in a very, very vulnerable position.

"Expose me for what, Danny? Having a rare skin condition?"

"I've got a vial of your blood, Sam. It's in a safe deposit box. If anything happens to me, my attorney has been notified to have that blood immediately tested. Your secret will be out. You will be exposed to the light for the freak that you are."

"Perhaps you should have already tested the blood, Danny."

"What does that mean?"

I stood again and removed a folded piece of paper from my back pocket. Earlier, I had stopped at a Kinko's and printed out Mel's emailed test results.

"What's this?"

"My blood test results."

"What the fuck are you talking about?"

"I had my blood tested, Danny. A variety of tests, too. The technician was asked to look for any irregularities. Look at the results yourself."

He quickly read through the report. Attorneys, if anything, were great scanners.

"As you can see," I said. "It says *no irregularities found*. My blood is normal, Danny. *Normal*. In every way. So have it tested. Do what you want with it. But I'm taking back my house, and I'm taking back my kids, and you damn well better believe that no sleazeball porn king who brings whores home to my kids will ever—*ever*— be welcomed into my house again. You have until eight p.m. tonight to move your ass out, and anything you leave behind will be trashed. Do you understand?"

He looked at the paper some more, then looked directly across at me, since I was once again squatting down at eye level. "So you won't report me?" he said.

"You disgust me."

And I leveled a punch directly into his groin. As he rolled out of the chair, gasping, I walked out of his office and didn't even look down at his bleeding whore.

Chapter Fifty-seven

It was 8:30 p.m. and Danny had just left.

I gave him the extra thirty minutes out of the goodness of my cold heart, since, after all, he had been working so hard to get his shit moved out. The kids were off eating pizza with Mary Lou, my sister. They would come home to find their daddy gone. Traumatic for them, I know, but they would adjust. They had to adjust.

Before Danny drove off, with his Cadillac Escalade filled with all his crap, he informed me that he had talked Sugar out of pressing charges, mostly by offering her a massive raise. I reminded Danny that I wanted a massive raise, too, in the form of a butt-load of alimony and child support.

As he sat behind the wheel, looking utterly exhausted, he leveled a glare at me that was supposed to make me curl into the fetal position. I didn't curl.

"This isn't over, Sam."

"I certainly hope not," I said. "I'm having too much fun."

He shook his head and drove off. I watched him make a left turn and disappear out of sight, and I realized I didn't even care where he ended up.

Smell you later, asshole.

I flipped the phone open and called my sister. "Bring them home," I said.

***

We were all eating hot fudge sundaes that were oozing with whipped cream and chocolate syrup. And, yes, some of us were only *pretending* to eat. So far, my kids had not caught on that I could not eat like them. Mostly, they just saw mommy not eating at all, and when I did, the spitting-it-back-into-a-cup routine worked wonders.

Even with all the spitting, some of the ice cream and fudge made it down my esophagus, which caused some seriously uncomfortable cramps. After a few minutes of pretending to eat my ice cream, I finally ditched the bowl and emptied the cup-o'-spit down the garbage disposal. Mostly, no one noticed me, and I just sat there, glowing, watching my kids eat ice cream and laugh with their aunt...in the comfort of my own home with Danny not watching over me.

The kids had asked repeatedly where their dad was, and I told them that it was mommy's turn to have the house, and that daddy was going to stay with a friend of his for a while, and that everything was going to be okay.

Tammy later came over and held my hand for nearly the entire night. She told me again and again how sorry she was for yelling at me on the phone. I told her again and again that it didn't matter and that I loved her with all my heart.

When we were done with the ice cream, I grabbed a clean comforter from the hall closet and we all snuggled together on the living room couch and watched an illegal copy of *Toy Story 3* that Mary Lou had purchased at a liquor store. I told her I couldn't condone such illicit behavior and vowed to purchase a real copy when the movie hit the DVD stands. Mary Joe stuck her tongue out at me.

About halfway through the movie, Anthony giggled. I knew that giggle.

"Oh, no you didn't!" I cried out.

He laughed harder and lifted up the comforter. "Dutch oven!" he shouted and a wave of stink hit us.

We all piled out of the living room, laughing and tumbling over ourselves.

And later, after the room had cleared and after we had finished the movie, while Mary Lou was twisting Tammy's long hair into a braid and while Anthony was showering, I found myself crying tears of joy.

Chapter Fifty-eight

It was the next night and I was getting ready for my big date. I didn't often get nervous these days, but I was nervous as hell now. And while I got ready, my AOL account twirped. It was Fang.

See you in one hour, Moon Dance?

You bet.

Are you nervous? he asked.

More than you know.

Don't worry. I don't bite.

I would have laughed if my stomach wasn't doing somersaults. I took a deep, shuddering breath. I really didn't need such deep breaths, but they did help to calm me.

How do I find you? I wrote when I had calmed myself down enough to focus on the keyboard.

Look for the man with a twinkle in his eye.

Smartass.

Trust me, Moon Dance, there will be no mistaking me tonight.

What's your name? I wrote. *I mean, your real name?*

I will tell you my name tonight, Moon Dance. Deal?

Okay, deal. I have to get ready.

See you in fifty-six minutes.

So we're really doing this?

Yes, wrote Fang. *We're really doing this.*

I shut down my laptop and went back to work on my hair. My hands, I noticed, were shaking.

***

I was driving down Chapman Avenue when my cell rang. I looked at the faceplate. Another restricted Number. At this late hour, it could only be a cop. I even had a sneaking suspicion who it was. I clicked on.

"It wasn't me, officer, I swear. Please don't use the rubber hose again."

"We don't use rubber hoses any more," said Sherbet.

"So what do you use?"

"Proper interrogation techniques."

"And if that doesn't work?"

"We dig out the rubber hoses." He paused. "Do you have a couple of minutes?"

"Anything for you, detective."

"I'll remember that. Anyway, we had numerous

eyewitness reports of something running through the streets of Fullerton a couple of nights ago, and I want your opinion."

"And because I have a rare skin disease and I'm forced to stay out of the light of day, that makes me an expert in all things that go bump-in-the-night?"

"Something like that."

"Was this *something* about nine feet tall and covered in fur?"

"How did you know?"

"Was there also a grave defiled?"

"Yes, over on Beacon Street, but—"

"Just a lucky guess, Detective."

"Don't give me that bullshit, Sam. What the hell is going on in my city?"

"You would never believe it, Detective."

"Try me."

"Soon. I promise."

He was silent on his end of the phone. Finally, he said, "How soon?"

"Soon."

He sighed. "I can be your best friend, Sam. Or your worst enemy. I have a city to protect."

"We will talk soon, Detective. I promise."

He didn't like it, but accepted it.

"Get some sleep, Detective."

"With a nine-foot creature running around? Hardly."

"You're safe," I said. "At least until the next full moon."

"You're shitting me."

"We'll talk later, Detective."

And we clicked off just as I pulled into the Downtown Bar & Grill parking lot.

Chapter Fifty-nine

I was in the same parking lot where a young lady had been killed not too long ago in connection with a case of mine. A case that had involved Kingsley.

The parking lot was mostly empty. It was late Sunday night, so no surprise there. I was in a spot that afforded me a perfect view of the parking lot's entrance.

I'm really doing this, I thought.

I was a few minutes early. To my right was an alley that ran behind the restaurant. The alley was clean and dimly lit and led to the back entrances to the stores that ran along Harbor Boulevard. Potted plants were arranged outside the bar's back door, and a nearby fire escape appeared freshly painted. The alley itself was composed of cobblestones, like something you would see in an English village. I remembered the way the girl's blood had soaked between the stones, zigzagging rapidly away from her dying body.

The moon was bright, but not full. Clouds were scattered thinly across the glowing sky. Glowing, at least, to my eyes. A small wind made its way through my partially opened driver's side window. I couldn't keep my hands from shaking, and so I kept them there on the steering wheel, gripping tightly, my knuckles glowing white.

A car turned slowly into the parking lot, making a left from Chapman Avenue. Its headlights bounced as the vehicle angled up the slight driveway and into the parking lot.

I'm really doing this.

I hadn't expected to be this nervous. Fang knew everything about me. He knew my dirtiest secrets. So what did I know about him? I knew he was a lady's man. I knew he had a massive fascination for vampires. I knew he was mortal.

And that was it.

In a way, I loved Fang. He was always, always there for me. In my darkest hours, he consoled me. He lifted me up and reminded me that I was not a monster. I shared with him my heart, and in return he accepted it with tenderness and compassion. He was the perfect man. The perfect confidant.

I didn't want to lose what I had with Fang.

The car continued moving through the parking lot. I could hear its tires crunching. The car, I soon saw, was an old muscle car. A beautiful thing. Not quite cherried, but obviously well taken care of. It gave off a throaty growl, not unlike the growl of the werewolf the other night.

I didn't want to lose Fang. I love what we have. Our connection was so rare, so helpful, so loving, so sweet, so important to me.

I can't lose that.

I wrapped my hands around my keys, which were still hanging in the ignition.

This was a bad idea. I should never have agreed to this.

"What am I doing?" I whispered, feeling real panic, perhaps the first panic I had felt in a long time. Far worse panic than when a nine-foot-tall werewolf approached me in my hotel room.

And what if Fang isn't who he says he is? What if he's someone completely different? Someone untrustworthy?

What if I have to silence him?

I started rocking in the driver's seat. The throaty growl of a muscle car reverberated through the empty lot, bouncing off the surrounding dark buildings. The car pulled slowly into a parking space two rows in front of me.

We were now facing each other. The windshield was tinted enough for me to have a hard time seeing inside. Still, I could see a single figure. A man.

The driver turned the car off and the parking lot fell silent again. A moment later, the muscle car's headlights flashed twice.

My heart slammed inside me. My right hand

was still holding the keys. I could start the car now and get the hell out of here and forget this night ever happened, and Fang and I could go back to what we had.

I could. But I didn't.

I reached down and flashed my headlights twice in return. A moment later, the muscle car's driver's side door opened. A booted foot stepped out.

Close to hyperventilating, I went to open my door but stopped short. Shit, I had forgotten about my seat belt. I hastily unfastened it and opened the door.

I'm really doing this.

As I stepped out of my van completely, the person opposite me did the same. The night air was cool. Sounds from the nearby bar reached us. Laughter. Music. The low murmur of a handful of conversations going on at once.

I stepped around to the front of my minivan, and the figure in front me did the same. He leaned a hip casually against the front fender. When I saw him, I stopped and gasped and covered my mouth with both hands.

Fang grinned at me. "Hello, Moon Dance."

The End

About the Author:

J.R. Rain is an ex-private investigator who now writes full-time. He lives in a small house on a small island with his small dog, Sadie. Please visit him at www.jrrain.com.